THE SEVEN

THE SEVEN

Steve Gladwin

Pont

To Celia, with whom I first discovered the grove.
And Rose, who loves it now as much as I do.

Published in 2013 by Pont Books, an imprint of
Gomer Press, Llandysul, Ceredigion SA44 4JL

ISBN 978 1 84851 743 1

A CIP record for this title is available from the British Library.

All Taliesin poem translations courtesy of
John and Caitlin Mathews, The Aquarian Press, 1991.

This book is published with the financial support of the
Welsh Books Council.

Printed and bound in Wales at
Gomer Press, Llandysul, Ceredigion SA44 4JL

'At last, in comprehension,
Not lost, we spake the Name.'

John Matthews – 'The Raid on Annwn'

ELERI

Tony Lewis ducked under the overhanging branch at the very last minute.

He didn't want her to see him – the new girl. He had no idea what made him follow her. Well, he did but it made no sense.

'This is Eleri.' Dizzy Davies, their useless teacher, had introduced her to the class. 'She's new to the village. Say hello to her nicely now, children.'

Typical of Dizzy to treat them all like five-year-olds.

The class had grumbled a response and Chris Lord, the class bully, had scowled at the thin girl with the long red hair and piercing green eyes.

Tony wasn't bothered that there was a new girl. He hadn't been bothered about anything much since his mother died and he'd been kept down a year. He felt out of place in his new class. Chris Lord had bullied him badly to start with, but now they had a sort of grudging truce – the boy from the caravan park with a drunken father and a mam they said was nuts, and Tony, the outsider whose mother was dead.

But there was something different about the new girl. Eleri wasn't like the others. There was something in her eyes which seemed older, wiser, and in the past few days Tony had the oddest feeling that she was just marking time, waiting.

He watched her, screened by one of the beeches on the way up to the Morgans' farm. Tom Morgan was in his class, but they didn't have much to say to each other. Tom was one of the rugby boys and they all spoke Welsh, which Tony was only just beginning to understand.

He was an odd mix, half Welsh, half Irish. Dad was Welsh but Mum had come from Ireland. They'd met in Yorkshire, where his dad had had a job. Tony had been born a couple of years later and then, five years after that, came his little sister, Sophie.

Then Dad had lost his job and they'd decided to up sticks back to Wales, to Dad's home village. But Mum had got ill. Seriously ill. Tony didn't like to think about it because they'd sent him away to his granddad's in Ireland. He'd been there at the end, though, holding her thin hand. There was nothing to her by then. 'Nothing but a bundle of dry sticks,' he'd heard his Irish granddad say when he thought he couldn't hear.

The alder tree had reminded him. That's why he was here now. Because of the tree. And because of Eleri. But though he had followed the new girl up here, he couldn't summon the courage to go any further.

He'd seen the tree down by the church. It had a sort-of face, with tiny dark knotholes for eyes and a long knobbly nose which made it look almost human. It sounded crazy but it was almost as if he'd seen Eleri's face there on the trunk. Another day it might have freaked him out, but today it made some weird sort of sense.

8

There was something about the alder and Eleri's pale face and red hair which seemed to belong together.

Which was why he'd run after her like some daft idiot and she must have seen him. But before he could call out to her, another voice beat him to it.

'Eleri?'

Oh no! Where had she come from, that pest Lucy Morgan, Tom's little sister, who was always sniffing and never had a handkerchief? Lucy with her blue-framed glasses which were always smeared with snot. Lucy who was always in a mood and who didn't have many friends.

'Where you going then?'

'Home.' Eleri didn't look best pleased to see her.

'You live up there, don't you?' Lucy's tone was almost accusing.

Tony saw the older girl turn to face her little persecutor. Maybe Lucy had seen something in Eleri's eyes because she shied away for a second, as if she'd caught a glimpse of the face behind the mask and hadn't liked it. She recovered quickly enough. 'Up there. On our tump.'

'It isn't *your* tump.' Eleri's tone was harsh.

Lucy just looked sulky at that and pushed up her glasses with two fingers and a sniff.

Tony was sure they could hear him breathing; he was still so out of puff from trying to catch up with Eleri.

'Well, it's above our house. No one ever goes there apart from our sheep and people taking their dogs for a walk.' Lucy was on the defensive now and had stuck her fists hard down into her pockets.

Tony saw the tiredness cross Eleri's face. It reminded him of his mother.

'I'm sure your house is very nice,' she said. 'And I'm sorry I snapped at you.'

Lucy's reply came out in one grumpy, breathless gasp. 'I've got to go and help bring the sheep in anyway and then it will be tea, and I thought you were going to be nice, but I was wrong because I can see you're really a stuck-up cow. And there's something weird about you – I can say if I don't like you going up to our tump and pretending you live there, can't I? – so you can stop, can't you!'

She paused. 'And you just tell me where you're supposed to live. Nowhere. There's nothing but trees up there and a new house that isn't finished yet. There's no —'

'Be still!'

It wasn't just Lucy that froze in mid sentence. Tony was shocked by the voice that came from Eleri. He'd been right. There really was something weird about her. 'Go on home,' she said in a cold voice, as though dismissing a servant. 'Go home to your sheep and your tea. Go to your white house with the hooks on the walls and old blood on the floor. Go to your dull parents and your brother. Go and leave me be!'

For a few seconds Lucy stared at her. Then she took off at a run back down the track to home.

Eleri stood with her hand on the smooth bark of one of the beeches. 'You can come out now, Tony Lewis,' she said softly.

Still out of breath, Tony ducked from under the branch and faced her, a bit shamefaced. 'How did you know I was here?'

10

'I could hear you breathing, idiot. Why are you following me?'

'Well, I'm not following you like she is. I mean Lucy's just a pest.'

'I shouldn't have been so hard on her.'

'Huh. I think she got off lightly.'

'So, anyway?' Eleri fixed those green eyes on him. 'What do you want?'

He didn't answer right away. He just looked at her for a few seconds. 'You're like no girl I've ever met.'

'That's probably a good thing.'

'No,' he said, a bit flustered. 'There's something about you that reminds me of my mum.'

He saw her face soften at that. 'She was a good woman, your mother.'

'How can you say that?' he asked hotly. 'You never met her.'

Then the new girl did something weird. She put one hand on Tony's forehead and pushed a stray curl away from it. 'Oh, but I have.'

Tony felt a fierce mixture of anger and excitement. Not sure which he should feel first. 'Mum used to do that,' he said, resettling the strand of hair.

'I know, Tony. Your mother and I were close.'

He looked at her as if she was insane. 'But how could you have known her? How? You're only —'

'Ten? But you know that's not true, don't you? You must have known there was something different about me or you wouldn't be here now.'

'That's not it,' he protested. 'I wanted to tell you about the tree.'

11

'Which tree?'

'Not sure I want to now. Do you expect me to believe that stuff about Mum?'

'You don't have to, Tony, but it happens to be true. Why not tell me about the tree?'

'It's going to sound daft, but then . . .'

'Maybe if you told me which tree . . .'

'Alder. The little one in the churchyard. It's kind of special.'

'Ah,' said the girl who didn't seem like a girl at all any more. 'The purple alder.'

'Dizzy Davies told us the Welsh name for it is *gwernen*.'

'She's right. So why is it special to you?'

Tony scrunched up his face. 'Well, er, I don't know, but just now I thought I saw your face in the trunk. Well, it was like you anyway but a sort of older version of you. More like, er, you are now.'

That was when Eleri beamed and squeezed his hand. She had a heck of a grip for a girl.

'What was that for?'

'Because that means it's time.'

'Time for what?'

'For the Seven,' Eleri said, almost in a whisper.

'Who?' Tony took two steps backwards. He was wishing he'd gone straight home, given the churchyard a miss and crashed out on the bed with his iPod. This was getting too much like a dream.

Eleri looked at him with eyes as old and searching as the sea. 'No time for that.'

'For what?'

But she had already grabbed his face in her hands. She pushed him back gently so that her hands were on his shoulders.

'What are you?'

'*Awen* inspire you,' she said and, looking deeply into his eyes, let out a single gentle breath.

Tony blinked and then took a couple of shaky steps backwards. The blood seemed to have rushed to his head as if he'd straightened up in a hurry.

'It's time to go home now,' Eleri said. 'It's time to go and look for the gift your mother left for you. Once you have found it you will be ready to sing.'

Tony looked at her without understanding.

'And I will be a good friend to you. Now go, Tony.' And Eleri watched the boy stumble away.

She stood there for a while, thinking, and then instead of continuing homewards she retraced her steps along the lane and through the back of the old churchyard until she reached the little alder bobbing over its stream. 'Thanks for looking after him,' she whispered.

And no one but the princess heard the tree's reply.

CHAPTER ONE

The Seven

It took a while for Tony to find the packet between two battered old trestle tables in Mum's studio. He had no idea what had made him think it might be up here.

Maybe because it was an obvious place if she had wanted to hide something. But then why would she want to do that?

It was the sight of his name that caught his attention. They were all packaged together in brown paper and heavily taped, but there was a card attached to the outside with a paper clip. His heart pounded as he glimpsed the message.

'Dear Tony,' it said. 'I can't be here to guide you any more but if you have found them then it must be the right time. Remember that I love you and I always will. X.'

For once he didn't feel like crying. He was too excited. So what had she left him then? It had to be paintings.

Tony pulled off the tape and unwrapped the parcel carefully. Then he lifted out the bundle of paintings and looked at them one at a time. There were seven in all. He thought he'd seen every one of his mother's paintings, but these? He'd never seen anything like these before.

They must have been painted as a set, for each one of them had a doorway in the foreground formed by a pair of ancient trees. Each of the doorways framed a different scene; they were weird. In every one, Tony's eyes were drawn through the arch of trees by a single figure at its edge.

In the bottom right-hand corner was his mother's familiar signature and then, in the top left corner of each picture, the same word, 'Gwern', in bold green. In the end Tony decided to spread out all seven paintings on the big tables so he could get a proper look at them and, as he did so, something else fell out of the parcel. Something which must have been caught on a nail at the back of one of the frames. Tony picked up the fallen bit of paper and looked at it. 'Come away from the fire, little Gwern.'

Tony sat for a while and stared at the paintings. He'd normally loved the things his mum had done. Not these though.

The images in the first two came from a chamber of horrors. A frightened little boy beating on the barred window of a damp cell, and a haunted-looking man crouched on a great throne and gnawing on his knuckles.

The third one was worse: a thin-faced guy in a grey-stained cloak. Furious, he was gripping the head of a terrified horse, pulling it away while others nearby neighed in terror. A knife glinted sharp in his hand.

In the fourth, a thin young woman with a red mark on

16

her face, eyes full of tears, fed crusts of bread to a bird which perched on a window ledge overlooking a grey and empty sea.

The fifth was gentler. A group of people listening intently to a tall, sad-looking man with a neat black beard. Feathers clothed his neck and he was strumming a jewelled harp.

The sixth painting was scary: a great steaming cauldron whose stink he could almost smell. Bending over it was an old woman with thin lips and cruel eyes. On the floor lay a child, whimpering, hands half covering his face.

The last one seemed almost normal. A man with anguished eyes and wild hair staring up into a tree.

Tony felt faint. What had Mum been on? How could she possibly have thought he'd like these?

All of a sudden he was gasping for a drink. He went across to the sink and ran the water until it was cool, and then filled one of the plastic cups. He drank it straight down, then went back to the paintings and saw what he had missed before.

There was a tiny figure in a yellow T-shirt and chinos in all the paintings. It was like looking over his own shoulder because for some reason Mum had painted him into every one of them.

Lucy might have forgotten everything if that daft young sheepdog Bryn hadn't decided to run away from the herd. Startled by the booming crack of a shotgun, he had taken off with a yelp while Dad swore and waved his stick. Her brother, Tom, had all but overbalanced on the quad bike, only just managing to keep the stock from scattering.

The gate was shut. The sheep were penned and safe but no one knew why the stupid mutt had taken off like that. Eleven-year-old Tom had for once been more worried about his tea than his dog. Which left Lucy, not yet hungry enough for birthday cake, to take off after him.

Eleri was right about Lucy. Behind the smeared spectacles and the snotty nose, there was a tough little warrior. But even Mam and Dad were astonished at the speed with which she took off this time. 'What's with her then?'

But they were used to Lucy and paid little attention until it was getting dark, and there was still no sign of her. Or the dog. By which time her birthday cake had lain untouched for three hours and Mam was starting to worry.

🌲🌲🌲🌲🌲🌲🌲

Lucy had got herself in a tight spot. She still had no idea why she'd chosen to go haring off after Bryn like that. She'd seen him run up to the little hill where the seven trees perched like old cocktail sticks stuck in an orange. Where she'd seen that Eleri climbing several times when she thought no one was looking.

No sign of Bryn though. Typical.

Lucy shrugged and decided to play her game. It was something she'd done ever since she could count to seven and she wasn't sure why. She did it at other times too but

18

always on her birthday. Counting the trees while she sang with her eyes tight shut. She didn't know why she did it and it made her dizzy every time. Count the trees, spin and see where the finger would point.

She gave up on Bryn and tried not to think about her birthday cake as she stood in the very centre of the green mound and concentrated on the seven trees. She opened her mouth.

'One
One-two
One-two-three
One-two-three-four
One-two-three-four-five
One-two-three-four-five-six
One-two-three-four-five-six-SEVEN.'

As the momentum of the last wild swing of her arms almost knocked her over, her pointing finger stopped at one of the trees. At that, seven sets of branches rustled in one united tree voice: 'Ask after the Seven.'

Without warning the wind took hold of Lucy but neither bowled her over nor swept her away. Instead it held her, picking up the spin that had left her pointing at the fifth tree, and turned it back on itself.

She spun like a top now but she wasn't doing it herself. She roared around in an excited scream as the wind took her up. She had no choice but to play the game and speak the words that had come into her head from nowhere:

'Who will take the Seven home
And bring the Dark Lord from his throne?
Who will show the Mage the skies

19

And bring the Bard an end to lies?
Who will raise the Ship again
And free the Princess from her pain?
Who will teach the Lost to fight
And bring the Child into the light?'

Lucy fell to the ground exhausted as the fifth tree swung open.

Bending her head carefully, she looked inside the trunk. The tree was a lot bigger inside than out. An arch gave onto a series of steps which led down to the floor of a great wooden hall.

Through the archway Lucy could see a mighty table with seven chairs of the same richly carved design.

At the back of the hall was a great door, heavily barred and bolted. From behind it came a roar which sounded like the sea.

Lucy could make out sleeping figures seated around the table. Great cobweb trails covered not just their clothes but their faces too. That made her shudder. Their clothes might have been nice once but were now only faded blues and reds and golds. Like something out of a fancy-dress shop, she thought, or some boring school production. They all seemed to be old men and no way did she want to disturb them. Just get the hell away from here.

It wasn't the sight of the old people in their faded robes, the oddly sweet smell that hung over everything, the sound of the sea and its distant, hypnotic up-and-down which made Lucy gasp. It was the two sparkling black-and-purple birds that flew above the company, circling round and singing the sweetest song she had ever heard.

She stood there, entranced, for as long as she could but in the end the heat was too much for her. It was like being in a greenhouse, like on their school trip to the Botanic Gardens. She'd hated every minute of it and the creepy fingers-up-the-neck feeling it had given her. She'd been close to being sick when Dizzy Davies had finally thanked the guide and let them out.

For a few seconds she stood transfixed by the birdsong, and then the fingers began their creepy passage up the back of her neck. She needed air.

She strode past the table with the sleeping old people and towards the bolted door held fast against the open power of the sea. The birds interrupted their song to utter sharp cries of warning.

The bolts at the top and bottom were old and rusted. She shouldn't have been able to do it but Lucy had strength as well as determination and was used to dragging the old barn door open when it didn't want to come. So she made surprisingly short work of this one. The bottom bolt was a lot harder than the top but it came in the end with a great tearing drag of complaining metal, gouging out the rotting wood on either side. She used all her strength to pull open the great sleeping doors.

Suddenly the singing stopped, drowned by the cry and roar of sea and wind.

The spell shattered behind her and the birds screamed. A dark-cloaked man with silver-black hair opened his eyes, blinked through the mist of cobwebs and ran

21

towards her furiously, grabbing at her shoulder. 'What are you doing here? It is not the time.'

Lucy just stood there, stunned. Scared out of her wits but horribly fascinated by the dark brown pebbles of his eyes and the deep scars down his left cheek. As she stared at him vacantly his grip on her shoulder increased.

She knew she'd done something wrong by the way the birds were flying round her head, screeching their rage. Worst of all, as she tried to move away, the man with the scar jerked her towards him. She could hear a dog yowling somewhere. Stupid Bryn. How had he got in?

Lucy's gaze blinked away from the man's face and towards the chance of escape. There was Bryn's howl again. Why, oh why, had she bothered with him?

'It is not time,' the man cried. 'Why have you come? You are too young.'

He had surprising strength and Lucy had used up all of hers. She had a sudden image of the rest of her family – Mam, Dad, and Tom – sitting down to tea. How she wanted to be with them!

Then an arm like iron was pulling her in and dragging her down furiously into a vacant chair. 'You will have to stay here,' said the scarred man. There was something in his eyes which showed that, even now, he was still half asleep.

'But it's my birthday,' Lucy wailed.

CHAPTER TWO

A Visit from the Butcher

Tony was helping to chop tomatoes and butter bread for tea. It was a good moment to talk about Mum's paintings. 'I've never seen anything like them, Dad.'

'So you said.'

'I'd like you to look at them. See what you think.'

'Can't say I fancy it much. Bit soon, you know.' Dafydd Lewis paused mid tomato. 'But I'll do it for you. So long as it's quick.'

'Or you could just tell me who Gwern is.'

'Gwern? Now, wait . . .' Dad had stopped slicing altogether. 'He was the little prince, wasn't he? Branwen's son. The trouble is I've forgotten a good part of the story. Comes with not paying attention at school.'

He paused to wipe off the excess spread on the side of the tub.

'Something about a fire?' prompted Tony.

'That was it. Branwen's son. Cast into the fire by his own uncle, Branwen's brother, and no one knew why. Mind you, after what the uncle had done to the horses . . .'

'Slow down, Dad. I'm lost.'

'Well, after tea I'll find you a book. If you're living in Wales you'll have to know the *Mabinogi* stories. Get you

23

brownie points at school. Useful for a *Sais*.' Pause. 'It's got pictures . . .'

Tony punched him on the arm. He was in no hurry to look at any storybook. He just wanted his dad to see Mum's strange gift.

🌲🌳🌲🌳🌲🌳

Dafydd Lewis looked over the bundle of paintings and sniffed. 'Well, to hear you talk I'd expected something a lot weirder. But no, I don't remember them.'

He held up the first picture and looked at it hard. Something was wrong. 'Funny sort of thing for her to leave you. They all seem pretty close to the story, mind. That book I'm going to find for you – it will fill in the details.'

Tony looked at the picture his father was holding. There was Mum's standard spidery signature – M.S. Logan – but now it had a different title. Not 'Gwern' at all. It showed a boy sitting on a three-legged stool with his hands on his chin. He just appeared to be bored as he looked out to sea.

Tony frowned, but let his eyes go to the next painting and then the one after that. They hadn't been like this before. These were – normal.

In these paintings the figure on the throne was playing a game – it looked like chess – with an unseen opponent, whilst the thin-faced man was stroking the horse's mane, as if soothing it. The bird had gone from the window of the third painting while the thin girl watched it fly off towards the setting sun. The man with the beard and the flashy harp just looked like a showy performer. In the sixth painting, the one with the cauldron, the old woman was explaining something to the little boy, who was nodding his head.

In the final picture, the man with the wild hair was in a boat in the middle of the sea watching a young boy fish.

'But – they – they weren't like this. They were different,' said Tony as his dad picked up one of the paintings and turned it clockwise as if that would help it make more sense. In none of the pictures was there any sign of an arch nor was there a boy in a yellow T-shirt peering through it.

An hour later, Tony was ready to give up on his book. It was illustrated and he'd expected to find it an easier read. He flipped through the pictures, drawn to one in particular.

It was as scary and powerful as any of his mother's. An illustration from the second tale, *Branwen*. The one with little Gwern in it.

There was a figure in the picture who reminded him of someone and he couldn't think who. 'Who's he supposed to be, Dad?'

Dafydd Lewis leant over his shoulder and accidentally spat crumbs. 'Mm, now, let's see. No idea, boy.' He shook his head. 'Whoever he is, he doesn't look happy in his skin.'

But Tony thought he knew who this was anyway. Efnisien. The one who'd caused all the trouble. The one who'd mutilated the Irish horses. The one who'd pulped the brains of the warriors in the house when they'd tried to trick them. The one who for reasons no one understood had thrown poor little Gwern into the fire.

But there had to be a reason, thought Tony. Why else would he have done all those things?

If only he could remember who the figure reminded him of.

'Whoever he is, he certainly doesn't look happy,' Dad repeated.

🌲🌳🌳🌳🌳🌳🌳

At school the next day, Tony couldn't get the sad, haunted face out of his mind. He'd understood enough of the story to know Efnisien died when he threw himself into the magic cauldron. He'd done it to break the cauldron's power and stop it bringing enemy soldiers back to life.

So in the end, Efnisien had given his life to stop the war. But why had he done all those terrible things?

Chris Lord! Tony gasped in the middle of stuffing his schoolbooks into his rucksack. That was why he'd had to keep looking at that picture and why it meant more to him than all the others. That was who the sad giant reminded him of, Chris Lord.

'You walking back?'

Tony looked up in surprise to see Eleri at his side. 'Yeah, OK.'

'Don't strain yourself.'

'No, that's fine. I thought you'd be walking home with Lucy.'

'She's not in school,' Eleri answered, wondering why everyone assumed she and the younger girl were joined at the hip. 'And I don't walk home with her. She sort of tags along.'

They walked in silence. Tony couldn't stop thinking about Chris Lord. How he never seemed to be happy, like Efnisien in the picture.

Something had taken the stuffing out of Chris that day. When she'd caught him with his head in his hands for the third time, even Dizzy Davies had been concerned. 'Christopher? Are you OK?' she'd called.

Chris's mumbled reply was unintelligible.

'Show you something if you've got time,' Eleri said, snapping Tony out of his daydream.

'Sure,' Tony answered. 'Where we going?'

'My house,' said Eleri with a grin, and brought out a bundle of keys. She began to twirl them. 'That all right?'

'Er – yeah.' What else could he say? It was all he could do now to keep up with her. They took the right-hand fork and then, having passed the Morgans' whitewashed farm and set the dogs barking, Eleri took the next right past a stand of beeches and an algae-choked stream.

'Bit of a climb,' she said, looking back at him, but still expecting him to follow. Tony trudged after her and tried not to complain. Half of him was working out how soon he could get away.

The slope up to the grove of seven trees was steep and Tony wouldn't have fancied it in the snow or mud. For some reason he'd expected to find a funny little cottage tucked in amongst the trees, but Eleri passed through them without stopping for breath. She climbed over a wall onto the drive of a brand-new bungalow and up to the front door.

'Watch your feet,' she called out as Tony stumbled over cans, bottles, piles of mail and a takeaway carton in the hallway.

It was dark inside and he nearly cracked his head on something. When she switched on the light, he saw that it was one of those clothes things that you strung up from the ceiling. It was full of blouses, socks and knickers. Blushing, he tried not to look.

'Come through to the library,' she called, kicking away at the rubbish as she went. Library?

To start with, the books were the only things he saw. Then he noticed a fitted gas fire along one wall and a socket for a telly. There was a three-piece suite and another little table piled with books and more dead takeaways.

Tony bent and picked up one of the smaller books. He read the spine. '*Triads of the Island of Britain: Trioedd Ynys Prydain*. Yeah right.' Then he looked inside and read aloud: '*National Library of Wales, Aberystwyth. Do not remove*. How many of these old books have you got?'

'You'd better sit down.'

'I can't stay long.'

'I'm not asking you to.'

Tony perched nervously on the edge of the chair. He flexed the big toe of his left foot, which he always did when he was unsure. He sniffed. 'Your parents don't live here, do they?'

'No one lives here.' Pause. 'I don't have any parents.'

'Who does live here?'

'No one, luckily. Not yet. The owner has been held up or something.'

'How do you know that?'

'How do you think? I've read some of his mail.'

At that, Tony tutted like a parent as if it was the most outrageous thing he'd ever heard. 'It's not your real name is it – Eleri? Where did you get it?'

'While that secretary woman was out of the room. There was a load of paper on the desk – old school lists. I picked the first name I could find. Then when she came back I made her think I was expected.'

'How did you do that?'

'Doesn't matter, does it? I did. Everyone thinks I'm supposed to be there and that suits me.'

'How long have you lived here?' said Tony.

'Since I arrived. No one knows. That's one of the reasons I went to your school.' She paused and grinned at him. 'That and to meet you.'

If Tony had been a cat she'd just sat on he couldn't have yelped any harder. 'Why?' Then, as if ashamed at being such a wuss, he added, 'Are you going to tell me your real name?'

Eleri picked up one of the bigger books from the carpet and flicked through it as if trying to avoid the issue. 'I could.' She sighed. 'I don't suppose it matters much now. Nothing's gone right, has it?' She looked straight at him. 'It's Branwen.'

'My dad's got an Auntie Branwen. She lives in Builth.'

'It's my name.'

'Then why don't you use it?'

'It's complicated. It would arouse suspicion. And there's someone I don't want to find me.'

'Who's that then? Is it something to do with those weird paintings of Mum's?'

Eleri grinned at that. 'You found them then?'

'Yeah and I wish I hadn't. Who are you so scared of?'

'They haven't come,' she said, ignoring the question and looking around anxiously. 'They should have been here by now.'

'Who?' Tony asked, even more puzzled.

'My birds,' she said. 'They should be here. They're my protection, see.'

A dark shadow fell between them and suddenly she was gasping in horror and scrabbling on her knees for the door.

It was then Tony saw him. The man. A huge man with a meat cleaver and a bloody apron. He'd appeared from nowhere and was towering over both of them.

Tony could smell meat and blood and death.

It wasn't the cleaver hand that the man raised. It was the other one, bunched in a fist and covered in dirt and ingrained blood. He gave a smile which was almost apologetic and spoke as if he'd been caught in mid sentence. 'It hurts me more than I can say, mistress. But law is law.'

CHAPTER THREE

Tony's Choice

He'd never been so scared in his life. It wasn't so much the cleaver-wielding maniac that frightened him. It was the fact that he'd come from nowhere, and Tony could see how terrified Eleri was of him.

The man tried to knock him out of the way to get to her. He was huge, and it was all Tony could do not to choke on the stink of blood that came from him. He shoved Tony out of his way as if he were no more than a fly that had landed on his hairy arm. He'd grabbed Eleri by the hair and now she was screaming – almost hysterical.

Tony looked around for something to whack him with. All he could see were books, but at least some of them were big. Almost without thinking he grabbed a large encyclopedia and bashed it uselessly at the side of the man's head. It just sent him slightly off balance and stumbling and roaring towards Tony.

'You can't,' Eleri screamed. 'He's just too strong.'

'Now, now, mistress,' the brute was muttering, as he steadied himself and grabbed her by the throat. 'I have to do it. It's my master's wish.' He drew back his fist again.

'Think of your mother's picture,' Eleri screamed as the fist crashed into her ear and her world went numb.

'Which one?' Tony called back, picking up the encyclopedia for another go. Eleri was falling, blood trickling from her ear.

He knew which one she meant. Of course he did. He thought it into his head as he heard the man mutter: 'A butcher's blow – every day straight from the chopping block – for the disgrace your people have brought to this kingdom.'

In his mind's eye Tony saw the sad girl watching the birds fly from her windowsill and the great grey sea beyond. He saw the poor clothes, the hollow cheeks and the red-rimmed eyes.

As the picture came into his mind he suddenly felt bathed in a warm, red-gold light. 'Mum,' he called out joyfully . . . and the butcher was gone.

He looked into Eleri's face as he helped her onto unsteady feet, and for the first time he saw who she truly was. Saw the same eyes that in the picture had been red-rimmed and full of tears, the skin that had been grey and sickly, the ear from which the red mark had run.

'Next time,' she said, wincing, 'you'll know what to do. Then I won't be deaf for the rest of the day.'

She stumbled forward, almost falling, so that he had to catch and support her. As he did so she gripped his arm and he felt how strong she was.

He opened his mouth to speak but she shushed him. 'Help me down to the grove. We should have done it first. I'm a fool.'

'What grove?' he asked her.

'The trees. The seven trees. You have to choose.'

Tony was puzzled. All he really wanted was to be home

in the warm, but he knew he had to help her. 'All right,' he shrugged. 'Tell me what to do.'

There was nothing to it as it turned out. She only needed to lead him from the cluttered house and into the near-darkness. He could still see the shadows of the seven trees, especially when she got him to stand in the middle facing them.

'My friends,' Eleri almost whispered, 'I have brought him.'

Maybe it wasn't just the sudden wind that made the branches of the oak, ash and beech shake. It almost felt like applause.

'Choose, Tony,' her soft voice urged him.

'But I don't get it. How can I choose a tree? They're just trees.'

'Look, I'll introduce you. Just put your hands on the trunk each time and say hello.'

They were by the side of the great beech closest to the bungalow. Tony could see the light behind him. He shivered.

'All these trees have names, Tony, but I won't tell you them now. There'll be plenty of time for all that later.'

Whatever that means, he thought.

'And if I did, it might affect your choice. You must greet them all.'

'Do I have to?' Tony felt daft in a way he never had with the alder in the churchyard. 'What am I supposed to do, anyway?' He liked Eleri but she kept saying and doing these weird things and, besides, it would be teatime soon. Dad had promised to call at the chippy on his way home.

'Just put your hand on the trunk. It's easy.'

'Yeah, if you say so.' In his mind Tony was already putting salt and vinegar on his chips. Besides, when he touched the first trunk he felt nothing. What was he meant to feel? It was daft. The whole thing was daft. But then he remembered the butcher.

Eleri watched, a bit like a teacher, while he put his hands on each of the trees. The only thing he noticed was that the two beeches were smoother than the oak and he could have told her that already.

But when he came to the last tree in line – the little ash – there was something slightly different. And that was hardly worth mentioning.

'Now you've met all of them, you can choose,' said Eleri.

'Can I?'

'But,' she put her hand gently on his forehead, 'first you must use that great gift of yours.'

'What gift's that?' he asked in surprise.

'Your voice, Tony. You must sing to them.'

'Me? Sing? You're mad. I don't sing.'

'Oh yes you do. *Awen* inspire you,' Eleri whispered as she had before, blowing softly on his face.

Tony began his song – not rock chant or classical string, or jazz twist or folk beat. It was something of all of them and yet none at all. It was newly minted and as old as the earth.

The girl had never heard anything like it. It touched her heart, reaching deep down inside her. It was a song like no other and it continued for a long time while she sat entranced, knowing she'd been right.

Without warning, the song was over.

'And now you are ready to choose,' Eleri smiled.

Tony blinked away the shock of the voice that had come from him. None of this made sense but he knew his choice had nothing to do with the pictures. Instead, when he cleared his mind the first thing that came into it was a memory of his mum. She was rocking backwards and forwards in one of those padded garden chairs that swung between two poles. In one hand she had an orange drink with a cherry in it, and an umbrella. She wore a blue all-in-one swimsuit and her dark hair was shaded by a big straw hat. She was smiling her smile. The one he missed so much.

Tony had one hand on the furrowed wood of the ash, the smallest tree in the grove. He didn't know why he'd chosen this one.

Suddenly tired, he slumped down against the trunk.

Eleri shook him gently. So he had made his choice. There were far too many things to tell him but they would have to wait till daylight. She would be safe for now but soon she would have to build her protection, and it wasn't easy without her birds.

She whispered in Tony's ear . . . setting him safely in the right direction. Then, because holding the spell meant effort and because she was so, so weary, she let Eleri slip away and now it was a princess who stood there in the middle of the green. A princess who lifted her arms to the skies.

A shiver of something in the night. Could her birds have come at last?

An owl hooted from the top of the sixth tree and then, as if suddenly startled, shook itself and hurried away, while she thought she could hear the tinkling strains of a harp, and behind that something deeper.

She stumbled home, tired, so tired. She shut her eyes against the dim light for just a few minutes and was about to drift away when it came to her. What she'd heard. The music was in the air itself and she could still hear it.

Eleri hurried back down through the almost black night and into the sanctuary of the grove, and as she reached the still centre she just listened, taking it all in like breathing. The music. The words. It had worked.

CHAPTER FOUR

The Grove Awakes

The voice rang out like a silver trumpet in the stillness. It was a private moment for a great bard who had been given back his voice, and for a princess who had forgotten to be scared for a while. The trees rustled and danced.

The bard's song continued for a long time. Tony was long in bed and snoring away by that time while his sister dozed in the next room.

Chris Lord was tossing and turning and trying not to wake his older brothers.

As Dizzy Davies dreamt of summer in her little cottage on the hill, the head teacher Mr Pryce's arm was stretched over his wife's shoulder while the twins slept like the little angels they weren't. Only in the white farm below was a light still on where a mother lay awake with worry.

At which point, the door in the fifth tree swung open . . . and Lucy Morgan stepped out.

She blinked in the darkness, the beautiful singing that had held her until now still spinning around in her mind. She had no idea of where she had been, or how lucky she was to escape.

Eleri went up to the wide-eyed Lucy and took her gently by the shoulders. 'You fell asleep,' she whispered softly. 'You don't remember anything else. Your family will be glad to see you. Go home now.'

For just a moment longer Lucy looked puzzled. She knew who this tall woman was and yet she didn't. She felt she should be mad at her. She was just so tired.

'And they've saved your birthday cake . . . and your presents. No one forgot.'

Still Lucy froze, as if unwilling to trust that any of this was true. 'But where's Bryn? He was in there too.'

As the music rose in a final great sweep Eleri took hold of her again, and, this time far more gently, blew into her eyes. 'Everything will be fine now, Lucy. You're home.'

The princess turned and pushed her so that she went stumbling down the hill, rubbing the sleep from her eyes and the cobwebs from a mind that was sure it could remember something strange, if she could only put her finger on it. As she fell, still dazed, into her mother's shaking arms, Mr Pryce slept on with his arm around his wife, while Chris Lord whimpered and dreamt of horses.

After Lucy had gone, the princess danced for a while; shivering and shaking beneath the trees, laughing and twirling when they couldn't. Despite everything she felt happy.

Then she heard it. A rustle of wings and that fluting, bubbling overtone which she couldn't mistake, and her face lit up with joy as at last two birds came and landed on her shoulder.

They were full of themselves in the way that only blackbirds can be. She stroked the feathers of each of them in turn and as she did so, she thought of Tony.

It took her a few minutes to realise that something else had changed and that she was no longer alone.

As the voice began at last to tire, she looked around her and saw them. They were still faint but she saw them, and knew they would soon be ready to take form. How she longed for the moment when the Guardians of the Cauldron would wake and start to put things right.

But not yet. Though her birds had returned and the boy had made his choice, the Seven still needed to assemble. Without the Seven, the Guardians wouldn't come. The boy was one of the Seven, Eleri was sure. Just as his poor mother had been. But where were the others? Who were they?

🌲🌲🌲🌲🌲🌲🌲

Tony had woken and now he couldn't get back to sleep. In the end he gave up and crept down to the kitchen for a glass of water, trying not to disturb Sophie.

As he went up the stairs to the second floor he noticed that one of the lights in the studio was still on – maybe Dad had forgotten to turn it off.

He ran up the short flight of steps and stopped dead.

She was sitting at the farthest of the long trestle tables; the one where he'd spread out the pictures. Mum.

Only this was his mum as he remembered her, and she was smiling at him. The paintings were in front of her. Her paintings.

People often wonder how they'd react to a ghost. Jump out of their skin and run away screaming?

Or maybe they'd do what Tony did right then. Feel a

warm glow that began at the base of the spine and then spread outwards. Because even if this was just some odd kind of waking dream it meant for a while that she was alive again.

There in the moonlight, looking like she used to look.

Maybe there are things you'd want to say to a ghost. All those questions about what heaven is, and can I put my hand through you?

Instead he asked, 'Why did you leave me those horrible paintings?'

His mum smiled in that familiar way, then she reached out one hand and gently stroked his hair. Neither her hand nor any part of her went straight through him. That was what made it even harder. That comforting hand was so her it made him burst into tears.

The ghost, or whatever it was, waited for his grief to pass but continued to smile at him. She reached out and wiped away his tears with two fingers of her left hand.

Maybe ghosts didn't carry tissues.

'That's what I need to tell you.'

Then it all came bubbling up out of him, all the things he wanted to ask and say. How he missed her. How they all missed her, and why did she look so well now, and shouldn't he go and wake Dad up?

She shushed him with a single gesture. She'd always been able to do that.

'You can't.' Mum shook her head sadly. 'If he came he wouldn't be able to see me like you do. Nor would Sophie. It's you I've come to talk to.'

CHAPTER FIVE

MUM

'Why?' Tony asked her – and there was so much in that one question.

'There's stuff I have to tell you and there isn't much time,' Mum said.

That shushed him.

'A few years before I met your dad I got this phone call asking me to do some illustrations for a book of Welsh stories. Well, this smooth-talking guy had heard I loved the *Mabinogi* stories and he thought because I was new and my work was popular with children there would be a market for something like it.

'Well, you know I'm a sucker for big projects, and the money was good. What's more, they gave me two years to do it in. I was only twenty-two.'

Tony listened, entranced. Ghost or not, Mum always told a good story.

'I had a few good ideas but none of them seemed to go anywhere. I just couldn't get any of it down and the two years just went and the money was running out and what was weird was that in all that time I'd heard nothing from the people who phoned. It was like they'd forgotten me, or I'd never even existed.

'Then, one night, this idea came to me in my sleep,

41

tumbling over itself to get out. Suddenly I was rushing down to the old shed at the bottom of the garden which I'd called my "studio" when I was a girl, and maybe that was all I needed because I could hardly get my old easel set up before the first one just came flooding out of me.

'Don't ask me how I did it. It was like I was possessed or something. By the time my father found me in the morning, I was fast asleep over the first of them. What I took to calling my "horrors". Well, you've seen them. I had no idea where they'd come from. They certainly didn't feel like me. I hated those paintings, Tony. I could hardly bear to look at them. And one after another and usually at the most inconvenient times . . . they came. Seven of them. Job done, hey?

'Then I met your dad and I was spending most of my time with him and only getting back home to Ireland maybe one weekend in four. One Friday I got off the train exhausted and I crashed out immediately. And then it happened again. Unable to sleep, then an idea coming which I had to get down. Stumbling down to the shed by torchlight and there it was the next morning, the worst one of the lot.'

'They're all pretty horrible,' said Tony without thinking. 'Sorry.'

His mum smiled. 'I meant the last picture. The eighth one. The Alder boy.'

Tony butted in. 'Gwern in the fire.'

Mum looked at him in admiration. 'Nice to see you've been paying attention.'

Tony nearly went to punch her on the arm but it didn't seem quite right with a ghost.

'Well, you know what your granddad's like,' she said. 'He took one look at that one and he told me I should bin the lot of them. Or better still paint over them so I didn't waste the canvas.

'But I couldn't. Not like that. I've never been able to waste work. So what I did was paint another set. Ones that felt more me, if you like. It wasn't as much work as you'd think because all I needed to do was adapt the others and make them – well, kinder, if that makes sense. And I didn't have much time for any of it either, pet, because by then there'd been a phone call from him. The man with the silky voice.'

Tony watched how her hands worked themselves in anguish in her lap. 'That must have been why I saw two different versions,' he said. 'The horrible ones you painted first, and then the others.'

'I was never sure I'd done the right thing,' Mum nodded. 'I had no reason either for hanging on to the others or fobbing him off with the new ones.

'The whole lot of the originals – Alder boy included – stayed in the studio in Ireland when I left and I thought that was it. Meantime I swore I'd never again have anything to do with anything Welsh. Apart from your dad of course,' she finished with a grin.

Tony stood with one hand nervously rapping the table. 'Mum, why are you here? And you're going to go away again, aren't you?'

She looked at him hard before giving an answer. 'Sweetheart, I'm afraid I can't really answer your questions.'

'Why not?' Tony asked, hurt.

43

'It's complicated.'

He opened his mouth but nothing came out.

Mum reached out her hand and squeezed his. She didn't feel like a ghost. 'Now,' – she gave him a sad smile – 'I have to complete my story. I don't have long, sweetheart. I wish I did.' She released his hand for a moment. 'I forgot about the paintings and got on with my life. Your dad and I got engaged and then got married and I moved with him to Sheffield and you were born and everything wonderful was suddenly happening at the same time. The original paintings stayed in Ireland for a while. I didn't want them but I wasn't going to let Dad destroy them either.

'I didn't recognise the voice on the phone when it came. It was soft and sort of correct this time. But the man was angry and he told me his clients weren't happy with the paintings. He offered me money to do them again. Somehow he knew that I'd changed them. He wanted me to bring them back to how they were. But I . . . I didn't know what to do. I didn't want to hand them over.'

'How much was he going to give you?' Tony asked eagerly.

'Fifty thousand pounds.'

'What?' Tony said, going weak at the thought of all that money. 'But that's crazy.'

'I know. Anyway, somehow I delayed him but he kept on trying.

'He phoned twice more, and the first time he got your granddad who you can imagine put a flea in his ear before he could even get to me. But the second time he caught me in Sheffield – I've no idea how he got the number – when your dad was out. When I finally told him "no" and he realised that I wasn't going to alter my decision he . . . changed.

'I would regret it, he told me. I was being young and foolish and totally ignorant. He had made me an offer far beyond the paintings' actual worth and I was insane not to see it. None of it made sense and his attitude just made me want to hang on to them more. That and the fact that I hated being patronised by some slimy toad like him.'

Tony had to smile – she sounded so like his granddad. 'You didn't give them up then?'

'The funny thing was that the moment I said no my career really took off. I was asked to do all kinds of exciting things and I couldn't fit all of them into being a young mum.

'I built up my reputation and you grew so fast and we were happy in Yorkshire with Dad working at the college. Then I got another phone call.'

'It was him, wasn't it?' Tony was getting ahead of himself again.

'No, you see the thing is I . . .' Suddenly Mum gulped and threw her head back in puzzled astonishment. 'No,' she said fiercely. 'Not now.'

'Mum, what is it?' Tony looked at her in concern; he could see that something was happening to her. It was as if she was starting to fade. When he'd come up here she seemed to be silver and strong by the light of the moon but now it was as if her face and features were wavering in and out, and he could no longer see her left hand.

'What's wrong, Mum?'

'Something funny in the moonlight,' she chuckled.

45

Tony wasn't getting the joke.

'I wasn't expecting this. Wasn't . . .'

Tony gasped as she let out a scream and threw herself backwards again. It was as if she'd been slapped. 'Mum, what is it?' he shouted, forgetting to whisper. 'What can I do? Shall I get Dad?'

'The silky man . . .'

'Who? Mum, tell me?'

'Him. The man with the silver-topped cane. Ohhhh.' She crunched into herself as if she'd been punched in the stomach.

More of her was fading and Tony couldn't quite see her face now. 'Mum. What do you want me to do? Mum?'

'Look in the pictures, Tony. Ask the princess.'

'Mum,' he pleaded, trying to grab her, to stop her being taken and feeling as if it was happening all over again.

'You must find the prisoner. The one hidden deep.'

'Who, Mum? How?'

With one terrible, tearing cry she was gone and, without thinking, Tony threw himself into the space she had left, fists flailing, roaring his rage and disbelief. That space no longer existed and, launching himself hard into it, he felt his head crack on the windowsill, and then there was someone else leaning over him.

'Tony. What is it?'

It was Dad, of course, face full of concern, his hair a mess and dressing gown open, and in the doorway behind him Sophie, one fist rubbing her eyes and the other clutched tightly round the ear of her favourite teddy bear.

'What is it, boy?' His dad frowned at him, his face crumpled with sleep.

'Sorry, Dad. Just a bad dream,' Tony replied.

'That brought you all the way up here. Was it those paintings? I knew no good —'

'No, Dad,' Tony interrupted him, horrified he might try to do something with them.

Sophie chose that moment to give a loud yawn, breaking the tension. They grinned at each other.

'Was it about Mum then?'

'Yeah. Yeah it was. Sort of.'

'We all miss her, boy. Now let's get something on that. You'll have a heck of a bruise in the morning.'

CHAPTER ONE

The Man with the Silver-topped Cane

Next day Tony woke with a headache and slouched off to school. He snapped at Dizzy Davies and knew he'd done poorly in his maths test. He couldn't tell anyone what had happened and even began to wonder whether it had. The look of pain on Mum's face when she'd been wrenched away from him had almost been worse than when he'd seen her in the hospital.

He was looking for a quiet corner after lunch, away from whatever this rotten world was going to come up with. There was a place he went sometimes, just the other side of the quadrangle and behind the old greenhouse in front of the school kitchens. No one ever came there apart from one of the school cooks to have a crafty fag. The last person he expected or wanted to see was Chris Lord.

Only this Chris Lord wasn't going to bully anybody. He was sitting with his back against the kitchen door and his legs up, whittling a piece of wood with a blunt old penknife. His other hand was clenched tight, his eyes were red and he'd been crying. He looked so sad that Tony couldn't ignore him. Besides he'd been seen.

'What?' Chris Lord scowled.

'Nothing,' Tony said. 'I . . .'

'I just want to be left alone. All right?' Chris went back to his angry whittling.

'Er . . . sure. Mind if I sort of sit here a bit?' Why had he said that?

'Suit yourself, Clogger. I'll shift up.'

Clogger! Once, Tony would have taken offence at Chris's teasing northern name for him. But now he was used to it. To his amazement Chris gave him some space. There wasn't much to be had but he squatted down, nervously wondering again why he hadn't just walked off. Neither said anything. In the distance a whistle blew and they could hear Dizzy Davies's whiny voice. The sound of football stopped until she had it sorted. Another whistle and the whole scatter of playground noise began again.

'Chris.'

When he looked up and scowled at Tony there was something half-hearted in it this time. 'What's your business, Clogger?'

'Just checking if you're OK.'

Chris stopped his whittling for a minute and looked up at him with dull eyes. 'Why should you then?'

Nine times out of ten Tony wouldn't have had an answer. He would have swallowed and stumbled and waited for Chris to get up and have a go at him. Only last

49

night he had seen and heard his dead mother and nothing was going to be the same again.

'Look, Chris, I don't know what's wrong. Whether – y'know – it's home or that kind of thing. And, y'see, I sort of get all that because – my mum – she . . .'

Tony couldn't say anything more. He didn't even know what he was saying. Why should he care how Chris Lord felt or what his home life was like? What was he doing here trying to help, apart from asking for a punch in the face?

Chris's response took him by surprise. First his eyes filled with fierce tears and he clenched both fists. Then his face got all hot and angry and Tony jerked back ready for the swing, kicking himself for having misjudged the situation.

Nothing happened. Just silence, before Chris mumbled: 'Thanks. Suppose you might understand. 'Cos of your mum . . .' He swallowed hard. 'When I got in yesterday there was something. Something on the board.'

'Is that why Dizzy Davies was asking if you were all right?' Tony leapt in, a bit too eager.

For a moment Chris glared at him. Tony jerked his head back but Chris just put one paw on his shoulder and steered him back. 'We're two of a kind, you and me, Clogger. It was about my mam, see. And this lot shouldn't know about her.'

'Sometimes they do though. Don't ask me how but they get to know. Maybe someone just heard Dizzy Davies and Prycie talking about you.'

Chris's eyes focused a bit harder as if he'd never thought of that before. 'See, Clogger, I loves my old lady and I hates the way they all treat her. Like she's crazy . . .' Chris swallowed as if he couldn't say it. 'And sometimes he beats her. It's not her fault, see . . . she's . . . special.'

Chris sank back, exhausted, and picked up the knife again. Suddenly his eyes lit up with something like pleasure. 'Tell you what, Clogger. I can take you to meet her. After school. You'll like my mam – and she's all right at the moment.'

Tony was about to refuse, all polite like, and find an excuse. Then he saw the need in his eyes and said, 'Sure I'll come, Chris.' After all, he thought, dead mothers in the night and now I'm friends with Chris Lord. Things can't get any weirder.

In the afternoon session they did some splodge-like attempts at painting. Dizzy Davies didn't know much about art and just gave them half-hearted enthusiasm as long as they didn't throw the paint at each other. Chris cast the occasional scowl in Tony's direction and pretended to give him the evil eye once just to keep up his reputation.

At afternoon break, there was a posh, silver-grey car outside the school gates and although Tony was no petrolhead, something made him go and look at it. Most of the kids were making their way into the playground to start another game of football and tear around or whatever it was they did. Chris was nowhere to be seen but Tony had a good guess where he might be.

A man had just got out of the car and was making his

way through the gates and up the steps towards the school reception area. He looked like one of the governors but there was something about him. Something Tony knew he should notice.

He ducked behind a railing. For some reason he didn't want the silver-haired man to see him. The stranger was wearing an expensive three-piece suit and shiny black shoes. The grey hat he wore was smart and new, as was the silver-and-blue tie with the fancy red clip. The whole outfit was completed by a black silver-topped cane. The only thing which didn't quite fit in was his hair. It was shoulder length and almost trendy.

A silver-topped cane!

Tony froze and felt a shadow like wings passing in front of him. A flutter of something just beyond his vision.

The man had pushed the buzzer at reception and was waiting for Mrs James, who was probably grabbing a quick cuppa.

Tony had no idea what made him go outside the school gate. Why he took such a risk when Prycie or Dizzy or anyone could have appeared any second. Fear? Instinct? A bit of both? The last thing his mum had done was warn him about the man with a silver-topped cane. This man. It had to be him. What was he doing here? Had he come for Tony?

He ducked down beside the car. If anyone came out now he could pretend he had fallen or something. He got up cautiously and peered through the side window. On the passenger seat were maps, sunglasses, an old chocolate wrapper, and a pile of business cards. He scrunched up his eyes and tried to make out the words. Hopeless.

Suddenly the football noise from the playground stopped. Something had disturbed the players. Was the man coming back?

Tony froze for a moment, his eye caught by a small white card face down on the pavement. He snatched it up, shoved it in his pocket, then slipped quickly round the corner and back through the side entrance.

He could hear the man's voice. It was raised, posh-sounding. 'Well that's a shame. I was hoping to see my niece. It's been a long time.' He was talking to Mrs James.

Tony thought fast. The man hadn't come for him but for Eleri. It had to be. How could he warn her? Instinct told him he had to find Chris.

He was back in his old place. A new bit of wood. No new tears but still the scowling red face.

'I'm not best for company, Clogger. I'll see you later.'

'No time, Chris. I've got a problem. Come on. We've got to find Eleri.'

CHAPTER TWO

Margaret's Kingdom

'There's this man at the front of the school. The one in the silver car,' Tony tried to explain.

'Yeah. Nice set of wheels.' Chris could see that Tony was shaking.

'Found you. We've got to get away . . .' It was Eleri, belting through the kitchen door which they weren't allowed to use and taking a step backwards at the sight of Chris.

'What's she want?' he asked in a sulk.

'There's no time to explain, Tony,' Eleri continued in panic. 'He's found me. We've got to get away.'

There was a moment when all three looked at each other, entirely different thoughts going through their heads. Surprise and confusion from Chris, and urgency from Tony. Eleri just looked scared out of her wits.

Seconds passed and they could see she was close to tears.

'All right then,' Chris said finally. 'We'll go to Mam. She'll know what to do.'

Tony could hear voices in the playground. Almost without realising, he found he'd reached into his pocket and brought out the card.

'What's that then, Clogger?' Chris peered at it curiously.

He read, slowly: 'Lord James Arran, dealer in anti—, anti—'

'Antiquities,' finished Tony.

'Come on, we've got to go.' Eleri gave a desperate tug on his sleeve.

Tony was gripping the card so hard he nearly crushed it. As he looked down at it he could hear the voice from the playground. Soft and cultured . . . and cold.

He felt the wings again and it was weird. As if a pile of bats or something had flown into his face and he was fighting them out of his eyes. His vision swam and he felt a sharp stabbing pain like a knife at the back of his head.

'What is it?' Chris asked as Eleri gave his sleeve a tug.

'Get us out of here,' Tony hissed back in panic.

Chris kept on walking, with Eleri and Tony following as he cut right through the ranks of caravans and plunged down an overgrown path which you couldn't see from the main road. At the end of the short lane there was a dead end, with the accumulated pile of vans and junk that was Chris Lord's home. Tony's heart felt as if it had crept up into his chest and he could hardly walk. How many miles had they run?

The place was a mess, a community of vans, most of them belonging to Chris's extended family and nearly all of them a scruffy peeling green and in need of a new paint job. One or two were uninhabited with just piled-up junk spilling out of them.

Chris pointed to one of the empty vans, a scruffy small effort which was lacking one front wheel. 'That's mine and theirs,' he said without enthusiasm.

'Here's Mam's,' he continued, and there was pride in his voice as he headed towards the one bright caravan with hanging baskets. 'I'll see if she's by.'

There was a decent patch of grass by the red caravan which they stepped onto while they waited. On it was an assembly of gnomes and toadstools in the same bright colours as the van.

Chris ran up the two steps, pulled on the door handle and then cursed.

'What is it?' asked Eleri.

'Locked,' he muttered. 'She never locks it.'

'Go away,' a shrill voice cried out at them. 'I've told you I'm not interested.'

Now Chris banged on the window before putting his face to the pane.

'You can bang all you like. I'll not shift.'

'Mam, it's me. Chris. I've brought some people.'

'Our Chris is at school.'

'Should be, Mam, but I'm not.'

'You're not him?' Her voice sounded scared now.

'No, Mam. Just open the door and you'll see.' Chris turned to the others. 'She gets a bit nervy,' he muttered. 'I dunno why she is now though.'

They heard the latch release and Chris pulled on it. This time the door opened.

The caravan was larger than it looked from the outside, fresh smelling from the bunches of herbs dangling from the ceiling. There were narrow bunk settees on either side and cupboard space above each of them with a small fold-down table in the centre. Behind them was a tall cupboard for clothes and a covered gas cooker and sink. It was all very neatly kept and its owner smiled at them through her broken teeth as she sat on the edge of one bunk with her son perched on the other.

'I'm Margaret, my loves, and you're both very welcome,' she said, as if she'd let them in right away.

Chris Lord's mum was older than you'd expect, with brown wrinkled skin. She was dressed in a bright yellow blouse with a red scarf draped round her neck, a darned grey skirt, long woolly socks, and white trainers which were scuffed, with holes at each big toe.

On the table in front of her she had a deck of playing cards which she was cutting as she smiled at them. 'Sit, my dears,' she said.

Tony hoped that Chris hadn't brought him here so that his weird mum could read his fortune. He wasn't sure he wanted to know.

Margaret smiled and said, 'You can fight it only for so long, love, but it will come to you eventually.'

Tony smiled at her in that polite way he smiled at his Auntie Gwen who was a bit odd and who only turned up at Christmas and christenings. 'I'm just Tony from Chris's class.'

All of a sudden Chris's mother grabbed hold of his hand and rubbed at it with two brown fingers. Tony tried to wriggle away but the strength of the grip surprised him.

'Interesting fate line you have there. Full of choices but you don't yet know which one to take. I could tell you, mind.'

Tony had just pulled his hand half back when she grabbed it again.

'A good strong life line. If you takes the right advice.'

This time she smiled and let his hand go and for a good minute or so afterwards Tony could feel a warm tingle where her fingers had been.

Now she smiled up at Eleri who, like Tony, was standing politely, waiting.

'And what name should I call you, dear?' Chris's mum asked her.

'It's Eleri,' she murmured, as if she wasn't sure.

Tony waited for Margaret to grab her hand too but she didn't. Instead she looked at her with her piercing eyes and then gave a sudden smile which lit up her face. 'Unknown you shall remain then,' she smiled. 'A good name to use, my lady.'

Chris looked puzzled and was about to say something but his mum got there first.

'Go and make some tea, Chris. And you sit, dears. Make yourself at home in Margaret's kingdom.'

Tony risked a look at his watch, hoping she wouldn't see him.

'Don't worry yourself about the tribe. They don't finish work until five-thirty and then more often than not they'll drink till they think their tea's on the table. We'd rather they didn't though, eh, Chris?' At least his loopy mum had let go of Tony's hand.

'Now then,' she muttered, shuffling the cards. 'Which one of you to deal with first?'

Tony tried hard to look at the floor, the hanging herbs,

Chris making tea, or anything else that would help him avoid her gaze.

'I've stuff to tell you so you'll need to get used to it. She told you you'd find it in the pictures so that's where it will be.'

Tony gaped at that, wanting to ask her how she could possibly know, but Margaret had moved on. Now she put her hand gently on Eleri's. 'My lady,' she smiled.

That was when Tony remembered. That Eleri wasn't just Eleri. That in some nuts way he couldn't understand she was the Princess Branwen of the story. The one with the weird brother who'd wounded the horses when he'd found out she was getting married, and whose picture reminded him of Chris.

The one who'd thrown Branwen's son, the little prince, into the fire before stretching himself out in the cauldron and breaking it.

The prince. Little Gwern. The one whose name his mum had put on those weird paintings. Why had she done that? And who was going to believe any of it? As if it was possible for some ancient princess to come back and be sitting here in this odd little caravan with the school bully and his mother.

There was no point looking to Chris for reassurance either because he was standing, cup in hand, with his mouth open. Then Tony saw why.

As Margaret touched Eleri's face there was, just for a moment, another face, another personality, swimming over and taking its place. It was Eleri but much, much older. The grown-up Eleri. Tony found himself thinking of the blackbirds and the butcher with the bloody apron.

59

CHAPTER THREE

In the Cards

Then as quickly as the change had happened, Eleri was Eleri again. Eleri who looked at Tony and gave them all a sad smile. 'He was sent,' she said. 'Sent to scare me. It is a show of power. A warning.'

'Who's he then?'

'Chris, help me clear this table,' Margaret said, cutting off whatever Eleri had been about to reply. 'And get the other cards down.'

'The special ones?' grinned Chris, as if they were sharing a secret.

'Those they can't abide,' Margaret smiled back at him. 'Help him, will you, Tony?'

He wondered why it needed two of them but Chris put one paw on his shoulder and led him to one of the cupboards on the other side of the van. The two women bent over their tea, talking in hushed voices.

'Shouldn't worry, Clogger,' said Chris. 'I don't get most of it either. I'm used to it. That's Mam.'

And that wasn't the only new thing to get used to, thought Tony. How come he was here with Chris Lord of all people? The school bully doesn't just become your best friend. It doesn't work like that.

But from the moment he'd seen the picture of the tall,

haunted-looking man looming over the cauldron in his dad's book he'd thought of Chris in a different way.

Tony helped clear away by passing things over to Chris. There wasn't much room. How could people live in this confined space, he wondered, remembering how big the studio was, and feeling a bit guilty.

'I told you she was special,' Chris said.

Tony just nodded. He didn't know what to say.

'We're safe now because I'm here and I can calm her down if she gets upset. She relies on me when Dad and all the others turn on her. But she can't go off the site any more because she can't cope with people. She says all their problems flood in and upset her, and then she has to tell them or her head will burst.' Chris Lord paused. 'She's different.'

'What about you though, Chris? Can you do it too?'

Chris gave him a hard, searching look as if deciding whether he could trust him. 'When I'm let,' he answered. Then with a satisfied grunt he brought up a small silk-wrapped parcel and took it over to his mother.

'And now, Tony,' Margaret grabbed hold of his hand fiercely, 'it's time to see if life and fate match.'

Tony wasn't into this at all, but Eleri smiled at him and he trusted her.

There was Chris too. He couldn't help his weird mum.

Tony watched nervously as Chris gave a sheepish grin and handed his mum the cards. She unwrapped the silk.

'Take the lady for a walk, Chris,' Margaret gestured. 'Show her the gnomes. She'll like them.'

Oh great, thought Tony. Now I'm stuck in here on my own with Mad Margaret.

'You're so fired up you'll be in flames next,' she said to him. 'Just relax and cut these cards. Your mum told you you'd find it all in the pictures, so what else did you think she meant? Those horrible paintings of hers?'

Tony gaped like a goldfish and then seemed to hear a familiar voice in his head saying, 'Shut your mouth. There's a bus coming.'

He looked at Margaret but she just smiled and handed him the pack. He sliced them down the middle and then did as she asked, turning the bottom half round and placing it back on the top. She shuffled the cards as if she'd done it a million times.

Margaret smiled as she worked the pack. There was something warm and different about her that made her look younger. She fanned out the cards until every one of them was visible.

'Think of the question you need answered most and keep thinking of it,' she smiled.

That was easy. He waited while Margaret shut her eyes and passed her brown wrinkled hands over the pack. He wondered again why Chris's mum was so old. She picked out the cards one by one, taking her time. She took so long that between the sixth and seventh he thought she must have dropped off.

Then her eyes snapped open and she drew in a sudden breath. 'There are eight cards here, Tony. These first seven represent the journey which you have already begun and must complete.'

Well that made sense, he supposed.

Margaret looked up reassuringly. 'The cards only tell you what you already know deep down. There is nothing magic in them. Nothing dark or nasty either, in case you were worried about that.'

He had been but wasn't going to admit it. Besides there was nothing scary about these cards. Just birds and animals. The first one was a hare in the moonlight, and the second a soaring eagle.

'Look at the pictures again, Tony.' Margaret's voice was softer.

Then a weird thing happened. One minute he was looking at cards with birds and animals. The next it was as if they had opened out like windows into another world. The original picture in the card was still there, but there was a second one in the middle of each which grew bigger before his eyes until it filled his vision.

Tony looked at them one at a time. The first image made him gasp. It was the figure of Mum last night in the moonlight, pale in its light and smiling at him. Within seconds he had changed his opinion of Margaret's daft cards.

The second image had only just happened. The man with the silver-topped cane getting out of his posh car outside the school. The one who called himself Lord Arran.

There was no way the third one could have happened yet but it reminded him of something. He was in a cold stone room with a kid dressed in rags. A kid who looked hollow-eyed and scared, but Tony was paying him no attention because his concentration was on a tall man with silver hair.

The fourth image was one he didn't want reminding of. Mum in the hospital bed all pale and wasted, her cold hand in his. All those tubes connected to her.

Margaret put a kindly hand on his shoulder.

'But that's already happened,' Tony cried in confusion. In the fifth picture he saw himself in the studio, poring over what looked like his mum's paintings. Maybe he was trying to make sense of them, he thought.

To his surprise, in the sixth he was in a place which looked like the grove. Was that one of the big smooth-trunked beeches on the end? If it was, he was perched uncomfortably in the hollow formed by one of its giant feet.

The last picture was an even bigger puzzle. He was standing with a little boy on a windswept beach. He could only see him from the side; the boy had golden hair which blew in the wind. There was a big rock looming behind them and the boy was excitedly pointing to something in the sand.

Now there was just one more card to turn over.

'Nice little tea party you're having here, Maggie?'

CHAPTER FOUR

The Tribe

Suddenly Chris Lord shot into the van like a scalded cat and it took Tony only a second to realise that he'd been shoved. He rubbed the back of his neck and looked to his mother, before his eyes flashed his alarm to Tony.

'What's all this old cobblers then? And what's the Queen of bloody Sheba doing outside? Come to join the gnomes, has she?'

Suddenly the caravan was full of hairy, sweaty men in stained blue overalls. The one at the front had to be Chris's dad: like him, but huge and hard-looking. The other two, clearly his brothers, were like stockier versions of Chris.

'Haven't I told you about messing with that rubbish? You'd best get the tea before you feel the back of my hand,' the huge man roared.

Then, to Tony's horror, he gave Chris such a hard shove that he sprawled across the table, scattering the cards and cracking his head on the shelf.

Tony saw how Chris was reduced in that moment. How all the confidence and happiness he felt with his mum just vanished. All of a sudden he knew what made Chris hate everyone so much, what made him a bully.

'Been to tea, have they?' The man's tone was bitter and sarcastic. 'Or maybe you've been filling their heads up with your nonsense. Has she?'

Chris's dad looked at his son as he picked himself up, careful not to show his pain. Chris began to collect the cards, trying not to attract attention. Tony saw that the images had gone back to birds and animals.

'Don't bother with that, Chris,' his dad said, snatching them out of his hand so that one of them ripped.

'Bin 'em. 'Bout time there was an end to this old nonsense. Does no one any good, Maggie, least of all you, eh? Here, go and shove these in the incinerator, will you? Then perhaps you can shift yerself and get some tea on the go for us starving menfolk.'

Suddenly he leaned right into Tony's face, smelling of stale beer, sweat and cigarettes. Tony tried not to wrinkle his nose.

'She's a bit touched is my missus. You don't want to take notice of nothing she says.'

'It's a school project,' Tony blurted out without thinking. 'We're supposed to work on it in threes. This is our, um, three.'

At which point the man burst into nasty laughter. 'Well you've certainly drawn the short straw. Getting saddled with this dummy. Hope you're not expecting much in the way of brains from him. Nice picture for the cover is about the best he'll manage. He can only just do joined-up writing.'

He laughed again at his own joke and Chris went redder and redder. Tony took a look at his watch and found to his surprise that it was five o'clock. Mr Lord saw him do it and sneered.

''Bout time for your cucumber sandwiches, is it? Well best get off and have them then, both of you, so the missus can get to doing ours. Go on – off your backsides and away with you. Chris, there's wood to chop. Go and join your mother outside. Get to it!' He moved to the caravan door, peering at something in his hand. 'Hey! Is this yours?' Tony saw that it was the card he'd picked up by the car. It must have fallen out of his pocket.

'Who's this then? Rich uncle? What's this antiquititis when it's at home? Some kind of disease?'

Tony picked up the card without saying a word.

'Cat got your tongue has it, Mr Lardy? You'd be singing from another bloody hymn sheet if you were my lad.'

'But I'm not,' Tony said, giving him a surly look as he grabbed the card, ducked under his attempted slap and ran out past him. He thought that was quite brave enough for now.

🌲🌳🌴🌲🌴🌲🌳

Margaret and Eleri were standing there among the gnomes and it seemed to Tony, blinking in the late-afternoon sun, that they'd been there for hours. The two brother gorillas had wandered off somewhere which left poor Chris in Margaret's van with his brute of a dad.

'We'd best go,' said Eleri, and she grasped Margaret's two hands in hers. 'Thanks for trying to help.'

'Don't go yet. There's stuff I haven't told you.' She looked back nervously towards the caravan where they guessed that Chris would be having a tough time. 'He was here,' she continued, pointing to the card in Tony's hand. 'And you know who I mean, my lady. He was here earlier and I'd locked the door against him when Chris brought the two of you. I thought he was back, see.'

'Maggie!' There was a roar from the caravan.

Tony shivered as he heard a thump, followed by a high-pitched giggle. He thought that might be one of the gorilla brothers. Poor old Chris. No wonder he was as he was.

'What did he want?' said Eleri, and the fear was back there in her eyes.

'You, of course, mistress,' Margaret replied quietly as she reached down into a huge sack of potatoes and dumped a load in the dirty old sink outside the group of caravans. 'Mind you,' she stopped and looked at Tony as she cleaned the knife on her dirty skirt, 'he was interested in you too.'

'Maggie – get to the tea, woman! You two! Thought I told you.'

Mr Lord ran down the steps now, a can of beer swilling over in his fist.

'Yeah, we're going,' said Tony with more confidence than he felt.

Chris appeared, carrying a huge stack of wood and trying not to drop it. His dad glared at him and belched loudly.

Tony wanted to shout at him so much it hurt, but they were on their way now. There was nothing they could do.

68

Margaret dropped her potato knife to help Chris.

One of the gorillas called out of the window of another of the vans. 'Aw, can't the dummy do it on his own? Does he need his mammy?'

Now Tony felt a fierce sort of anger of the kind he hadn't felt since after his mum died. Eleri tugged at his sleeve.

Margaret called after them as they ran down the narrow path and towards the main entrance. 'Be careful, dears. He will come sooner than you think.' Then before she bent back to her task, her rough hands stroked the back of her son's head.

Tony was still shaking when they got back to Eleri's bungalow. The place was still a mess. 'Poor old Chris.'

As they settled down on the old sofa in the cluttered library it began to rain.

'Good job we're inside,' Tony said. 'Left my coat in school.' Then, after a pause, he added, 'So are you going to tell me what's really going on?'

Eleri smiled. 'I thought you were going to tell me about the cards.'

'Well, I'm not. Not until you tell me the truth. You're supposed to be my friend. Whoever else you are.' He felt weird saying it.

She sighed. 'It's not easy.'

'I saw my dead mum last night,' Tony said. 'That wasn't exactly easy either.'

CHAPTER FIVE

The Keepers of the Cauldron

Eleri rose with a sigh and began to walk up and down the room. She picked up one of the books and flicked through it. Then she perched on the arm of the sofa.

'You know who I am?' she asked softly.

'Yeah but until I saw that butcher bloke I wouldn't have believed it.' Tony gave a shiver as he remembered it.

'I don't know exactly why I'm here this time.'

'What do you mean *this* time?'

'I'm sorry. It's not easy to explain.'

Tony almost snorted. 'Yeah right. You come to my mum in her dreams. And you're telling me you don't really know what's going on?'

Eleri gave him a pained smile. 'I didn't explain that very well, did I? What I'm trying to say is that I am here for a reason, but I don't yet know what that is.'

'Uh?'

'OK, put it another way. You understand how sometimes people can be put to sleep. For a long time. And then when they're ready, they wake up. When the time is right?'

'Sure.' Tony shrugged.

'Then just think of that as what happened to me. I went to sleep. And when my time came I woke up. And that time is now.'

OK, Tony thought. He could just about accept it. 'So you're saying Branwen never really died?'

'No.' She shook her head. 'I'm saying that I have been sleeping. For a long, long time. But now I'm needed, I've woken up. Me and the others.'

'But the story said you were dead,' Tony insisted. 'Your heart was broken.'

'Thanks for reminding me.' Eleri gave him a direct look. 'Listen, Tony,' she grinned. 'It's all far too complicated and you had enough trouble with the trees!'

That made him laugh and broke the tension a bit.

'And,' she added with a sigh, 'I haven't time.'

Without knowing why, he shivered and gave a nervous glance behind him.

'He's bound to try again. He's not the sort to give up.'

'The man with the silver-topped cane, you mean?'

Eleri winced. 'Lord Arran he calls himself this time. "Keeper of Antiquities". Isn't it funny how people never make much effort to disguise their name?'

'I don't get you.'

'OK, Tony. I need to tell you about the cauldron. Because that's what all this is about.'

'The one in the story? Your story, I suppose.'

'Tell me what you remember about it.'

Tony shrugged. 'Not a lot. It's what they fought over – the Irish and the Welsh. But I don't get why. I mean I know it could bring the dead back to life and I suppose that's pretty cool but . . .'

'It was even more powerful than that, Tony. If it got into the wrong hands it could do untold damage. We only realised when it was too late. Now tell me what you remember about the end of the story. After the battle.'

'Yeah, well, that's the weird bit. I mean, Brân cutting off his head and having it sing to his followers for eighty years. As if.'

Eleri put up her hand to stem his flow. 'What if there was a weapon, Tony, that was so hot you daren't touch it? What would you do?'

'I dunno,' he shrugged, not really making an effort. 'Find some way of cooling it down, I suppose.'

'So imagine the red-hot thing is a cauldron. What then?'

Then he got it. 'That's what the eighty years was about then. Making it safe.'

She nodded. 'But it went wrong,' she said. 'One of my brother's followers opened the door to the west and the spell was broken.'

'Bet he was popular!'

'It meant the end of everything. It meant that he had to die and so there weren't seven any more. It meant that the cauldron hadn't been healed. That the magic was incomplete.

'But there was one thing that could make it safer. Brân had requested that his followers bury his head at the White Mount. That's the place you now call the Tower of London. Have you ever wondered why it's ravens that guard it?'

Tony hadn't.

'Well, *bran* is the word for "crow". Brân would be able to protect the land while his head was buried there. The cauldron had been returned to its rightful guardian. No one could work mischief with it.'

'So did someone steal it back?'

'I'll come to that.' Eleri patted his shoulder. 'A new king thought that he could do a better job of protecting the land. Not some daft old legend of a buried head. King Arthur. He was the one who dug up Brân's head.'

Tony jumped up in excitement. 'King Arthur? Really?'

'But not the king you think you know. The next thing he did was go and steal the cauldron back, and I can't tell you what trouble and suffering that caused.'

'But what about you? How are you involved in all this?'

'When everything had been put right again, and the head was back where it should be, seven people were charged with guarding the cauldron. The seven who in turn would wake if someone threatened to use the cauldron's power.'

'And that someone is,' Tony butted in eagerly, 'that man. Lord Arran.'

Eleri nodded.

'And how do you – we – stop him?'

She sighed. 'It's not that simple. But I will try to explain. There are seven Guardians of the Cauldron, but also one called the Waker. The Waker isn't one of the Guardians but is appointed to wake them when the time is right.'

'You?' Tony guessed.

'Me, Tony. But at the same time, once the Guardians

are assembled, there are others in this realm bound to serve them in their great task. There are seven of them too. One for each of the Guardians.'

'What do they do then? The Seven?'

'Their task is to assist the Guardians.'

A flash of realisation crossed Tony's face. 'I suppose you're going to tell me . . .'

'That you are one of those brave unfortunates,' said a deeper voice.

Tony jumped then gasped.

The voice continued: 'Along with poor dear Margaret and her clod of a son. And one or two others who I have yet to prise out of the woodwork. But you can be certain I will.'

The man who called himself Lord Arran was standing with them. The wind and rain lashing the windows had masked the sound of his approach. He was still carrying the silver-topped cane which he rapped twice on the floor. 'I didn't find you earlier, my dear, so I'm pleased that you are here now. And as for this resourceful young man, it would be nice to say that the pleasure is all mine.'

'Why should I have anything to do with the man who killed my mother?' Tony said.

The other's face darkened and lost the fake charm very quickly. 'Alas nothing is ever as simple as we think. But I would strongly advise you not to cause me any more inconvenience. I've already had enough trouble from your family. How are your father and Sophie? Well, I hope.'

Eleri remained silent but Tony clenched his fists. He was about to say or do something more when there was a great crash of lightning and a joyful voice filled the room:

> *'Here is a Bard who has not chanted yet,*
> *But he will sing soon,*
> *And by the end of his song,*
> *He will know the starry wisdom.'*

'More trouble,' said Lord Arran. 'Oh dear.'

CHAPTER SIX

THE GATHERING

After Tony and Eleri had left, Chris and his mum set to doing what they normally did, which was keeping out of the way. Margaret hadn't meant to end up living on a dump of a caravan site with a husband she hated. She only stayed because of her youngest son.

While Chris chopped up the wood which his dad and brothers would sell to the local farmers, Margaret peeled potatoes and scrubbed carrots and diced swede and turnip. A broth made of onion, garlic and a secret combination of herbs learnt from her grandmother simmered away in the huge old cauldron and three young rabbits had been skinned and cleaned on the chopping board. She hummed an old tune to herself as she prepared the food and looked across at her child and wondered how she would tell him about what might happen.

When the man had come earlier on that afternoon she had had the wild urge to tell him everything she knew. Maybe if she had he would have rewarded her and found somewhere safe for her and Chris to go.

She hadn't of course. She'd pretended to be the mad woman in the van everyone thought she was, including her husband and two elder sons.

She thought he'd been taken in. She'd felt his subtle probing and knew how dangerous he was. She'd made sure he got nowhere. She had enough in her to hold him back for a while.

♣♠♦♣♦♠♣

Two miles away, that same man stood in a moonlit bungalow listening to the joyful deep voice that thundered from the trees. He could do nothing to stop it and he knew it.

Eleri stood and held the boy's hand protectively and shouted back her joy. 'My friend,' she called out into the night. 'You are welcome in the grove. The Waker calls to you. Here is a bard who is ready to chant.'

Tony had only just held himself back. He wasn't going to let his mother down. As the booming voice continued, the walls and floor shook and Tony, taken by surprise, reached out for the nearest thing to support him, which happened to be Lord Arran.

He felt a great jolt go through him like electricity, but more thrilling than painful. A feeling of power. He saw the look on Lord Arran's face as if he too had recognised something unexpected. Then as the force of the storm and the voice outside combined, the bungalow shook itself like some great dog after a bath and Tony was sent sprawling to the floor. As he righted himself again he caught hold of Lord Arran's arm to steady himself and grabbed at his hand.

A bolt of pure white light shot through the window between the two struggling figures. The great voice halted for just long enough to register its surprise and Tony . . . connected.

He was standing in a tiny white place of damp cold stone, hearing the moans of the wind and the creak of the old castle around him. He had a clear view of the sea through a poky window which had two great bars crossing it.

And then he saw him, the little boy dressed in a ragged shirt and trousers. 'Is it you?' the thin child whispered.

'Yes,' Tony replied. Although he wasn't sure that he was.

'Then will you help me? Please?' the little voice pleaded.

'But what can I do?'

'Sing,' said the boy. 'Sing for me.'

And then, without intending to, Tony opened his mouth and that glorious stream of song poured out for the second time.

Margaret Lord was ladling out the rabbit stew onto the cracked old china plates that had been worth something until Perry had started ruining them one by one in the microwave. Chris sawed off hunks of bread with a knife which badly needed sharpening and swore as he nicked his finger. In only a couple of minutes the beasts would descend again.

'Careful, love,' she checked him, but he just grinned and sucked hard. You had to be tough to be a Lord.

She looked down at the heaped plates and saw that Allan had more rabbit on his. If she wanted trouble and fists before midnight that was the way to go about it. She was just transferring some stew between their plates with a spoon when it hit.

Nothing in the world could ever have prepared her for it. It wasn't like the gift, which she had had since she was a girl, and which, like her mother and grandmother before her, she had learnt to cope with. This was a feeling of such pure joy that she could hardly speak.

She looked across at Chris who'd been shining the cutlery on a dirty old cloth and saw the look in his eyes. He was feeling it too.

They exchanged one astonished glance . . . as if they were truly seeing each other for the first time, and then set off through the rain. One minute it was a bright autumn evening; the next a deluge of a storm with growling thunder and punishing rain.

The boys were already rolling out of the far caravan where they kept their scrumpy and heading for their rabbit stew and doorstops of crusty bread in the rain but there would be no one to serve it. They shouted out their anger as they came but no one took any notice.

They ran on through the night, mother and son. She with her apron still flapping uselessly where she had part untied it; he still carrying his dirty cloth. As if they'd had no time for anything apart from obeying the call. Margaret's old trainers flapped as she ran and Chris's huge feet pinched in his brother's hand-me-down shoes, which were too small for him. Neither of them either minded or noticed.

Down the path and back onto the main road of the park they ran and narrowly missed being mown down by a pair of cyclists.

'Idiots.'

They covered the remaining two miles in just under a quarter of an hour and although Chris got an agonising stitch as they were running back over the bridge, he still kept on. It was a call he was powerless to ignore.

Margaret had never been to the place apart from in her dreams; while Chris had been there many times, though all he remembered was the occasional flashback. A tree with its shattered branch lying on the ground like a failed knight after a joust. More often he had the dreams he hated most. The ones where he was hurting his beloved horses.

🌲🌲🌲🌲🌲🌲🌲

From the window of the bungalow, Eleri could see two new figures in the grove, shivering in the lashing rain.

More familiar were the two leaping over the woodland stile and heading down to join them.

Normally the appearance of a lank-haired middle-aged woman in trainers and a hulking boy in a faded tracksuit might have been a source of amusement but seeing these two just made her smile.

Lord James Arran stood dazed and rigid in the middle of the room.

Eleri ignored him and grabbed hold of Tony who was still singing, his face lit with joy and his voice clear and gleaming like crystal.

As she pulled him out of the front door and into the lashing rain he stopped singing for long enough to shout at her over the roar. 'Why didn't you tell me it was going to be now?'

'Because I couldn't be sure. I still can't. There are still things that aren't complete.'

Margaret Lord put a gentle hand on her son's shoulder and steered him into the centre. There was a look of wonder on his face like she'd never seen. She looked down at herself and noticed the flapping apron for the first time. She shook it off and left it there, the pelting rain already soaking it. She took her son by the hand and walked towards the two others. They stood looking up at the trees, which shook and shivered in the face of the storm.

'Good evening,' laughed the man in the soaked tweeds, and held out his hand. 'A fine evening for it, isn't it? I'm Edwin by the way. Edwin Storr.'

The man with him must have been half his age, tall with long blonde hair that slapped into his face in the wind. 'I don't really do handshakes,' he smiled. 'But I'm Lew. Lew Gardner.'

Margaret took one hand and gave the blonde-haired man a clumsy hug, which seemed to please him a lot. 'I'm Margaret,' she said. 'And this here is Chris.'

'Lovely,' said Edwin. 'Now I think we should get ourselves under some shelter. Don't you?'

There was a look of wonder on Eleri's face as the twin voices continued to ride the storm. She looked around her at the two strangers, and at the shivering figure of Chris, and Margaret in her flapping trainers. Then she looked at Tony with his eager bright eyes and his glorious voice and smiled.

She saw without surprise that everyone was finding their way to their special tree. There under the furthest of the great beeches stood a tweed-clad man with a shock of wild white hair and a great beak of a nose. Almost opposite him under a tall oak was a young man dressed in a coat and trousers of many colours. Margaret Lord, for all her trailing shoelaces, looked like she belonged under the second beech with its enormous feet. Poor Chris looked thoroughly confused for a while, trying briefly to join his mother in the shelter of her tree while he got progressively wetter.

'Where, Mam?' he shouted out into the storm. Then some instinct led him to the third tree with its shattered branch.

The others would come, Eleri thought, as she looked at the unoccupied trees.

Eleri found further delight as her birds flew down to her but instead of landing arguing on her shoulder as normal, their flight was high and erratic. At first she thought they must be struggling in the wind but there was more to it than that. They were clearly distressed, chirruping at her and each other in urgent voices.

'Calm down,' she smiled at them. 'I know it's exciting. We've been waiting such a long time.'

The booming voice cut across the storm, but this time it spoke rather than sang. Was that a note of warning? 'The Guardians will come when the Seven are gathered.'

But there aren't seven of us yet, thought Tony. Surely that had to make a difference?

CHAPTER SEVEN

THE WRONG SEVEN

For a few seconds it seemed as if it would be all right. Tony could see shapes beginning to form around each of the trees, so that they were almost part of the tree itself. He could only make out odd bits of them here and there but he felt a surge of excitement.

Then a sudden, cold wind fell among them that went through him like ice. He stopped singing as all the joy dropped out of him. As he watched, in the very centre of the grove, a new group of figures was forming, blurry at first, but then bit by bit becoming more solid. The shapes they took were strong and proud, their faces noble but their features gaunt.

Tony frowned. These figures were wrong. They wore garments of faded red and gold, of dull green and a blue that had lost its sheen.

The one who spoke was hooded in a cloak of brown and grey. He threw it back to reveal a dark handsome face with a brown beard shot with silver. He reached scarcely medium height but wore a sword far bigger and more impressive than the others. He gave a bow which was both formal and cold. 'We have been summoned and must come.'

Eleri sank to her knees as if she had lost all of her strength. Fighting back panic, she was gazing, horrified, at the warriors in the centre of the grove. The excited song of the blackbirds on her shoulder had turned to agitated squawks.

'What have you done?' she gasped and Tony saw her stagger to her feet. Why was she pointing at him?

Tony felt himself getting angry. Angry at her. Angry at this rotten storm. Angry at being soaked through and miserable. Thanks, Eleri. Thanks a bunch. 'I didn't do anything.'

'But you must have done,' Eleri cried in panic.

Tony didn't understand. What was he supposed to have done now?

When he looked at the trees the half-formed shapes had gone. Only the warriors remained. 'Who are these?' he gasped again.

'Arthur and the others who stole the cauldron,' moaned Eleri in desperation.

'Is that a bad thing?' asked Tony with the horrible feeling that it was.

His question was answered as he felt a biting wind sweep through the grove again but this time he knew where it had come from. From the cold king and his small army of chill warriors.

'Once they are summoned,' Eleri said, 'they cannot return without taking someone back with them.'

'But I didn't summon them.'

'Somebody must have.'

Just for a few seconds it felt like when Mum and Dad

used to row and neither one was wrong. He might have laughed, but cried out instead.

Too late to prevent the great sweep of the king's sword mowing Eleri down in one vicious swipe. As she fell, Tony saw the figure of Lord Arran standing over her. Released from whatever spell had held him, he had discarded the hat and jacket and was dressed all in black. His white hair seemed to have grown longer so that it reached past his shoulders. He looked taller too.

Tony made as if to confront him.

'Far too late for any of that, I'm afraid,' Lord Arran said and nodded to the king.

All of a sudden Tony saw the warriors as they truly were. The vicious scars, the missing eye, the teeth worn in a necklace. He wanted to help Eleri up but the warriors were crowding around her.

He was on his feet and rushing at them hopelessly. He had to try for her sake.

Chris, Margaret and the others stood there, rigid and useless. Only Tony could help. Not for long. Something cold and hard smashed into the side of his head and he fell down into darkness.

PART III
EDWIN

CHAPTER ONE

RETURN

Tony reached into the rucksack he had grabbed on his way out, fighting the string fastening to loosen it, stuffing in the sandwiches and drink his dad had insisted on.

After the blow to the back of his head, his memory was fuzzy. Had he dreamt it all? With Eleri gone there was only one person he could ask. Chris's crazy mum had seemed to know things, and she had shown him those cards. He'd just have to go up to the site to see her, and hope the gorillas were at work. Or perhaps he'd dreamt all that as well.

Dad hadn't been happy about it so soon after. 'You ought still to be resting, boy. It's barely a week.'

Meaning since last Saturday morning when he'd dragged himself home after waking up soaked in the grove. Dad had been about to phone the police when Tony stumbled in full of apology and shaking his way into a bad dose of flu. He'd spent the week off school recovering and even now felt a bit shaky.

Now, with a fifty-minute wait before the bus, he made his way carefully up to the grove and tried to piece together what he remembered about that lost night.

Then under the shade of the tree canopy he felt the chill of autumn and was glad he'd worn a coat. He stood there in the centre and looked around for any sign that could help him.

As his mind cleared he remembered touching Lord Arran's hand which was when he'd seen the character in Mum's first picture. The boy trapped in the castle underneath the sea.

He remembered the sorrow and despair of a little boy who didn't understand why he'd been trapped and imprisoned.

There was something else he needed to recall. Something he hadn't been able to see or hear as the storm had raged and two voices had soared into the grove, his own silver pure, the other bass and root deep.

That look of triumph on Lord Arran's face, as if things had turned out just as he'd wanted.

And somehow it was Tony who had done it. Brought Arthur and the warriors to the grove. Brought the warriors who had taken away poor Eleri. God knows where she was.

So now it was up to him to put it right.

He heard the whimper a couple of times before he took any notice.

Beneath one of the great beeches a pitiful sight greeted him. All skin and bone and with his coat matted from too many soakings, a dog was huddled, whimpering so softly, if it hadn't been a windless day he

88

would have missed it. It was a sheepdog and it was in a sorry state.

Tony bent down and stroked the animal's head. It looked up at him with soulful and trusting brown eyes and a daft, lopsided look. One of its ears refused to sit up and just flopped over like an old chewed teddy bear's.

He gathered the dog up gently in his arms, shocked by the bones sticking through its fur. His hands found the tag around its collar.

Bryn. Pen Coed Farm.

He had only half an hour before the bus but he knew what he had to do.

It took him a while to raise any of the Morgans but in the end it was the barking of the other two farm dogs, surprised and delighted by the return of their missing companion, that brought someone out.

Tom was carrying a fork for the hay. He grinned at Tony and shouted at the dogs to be quiet. 'What you got there?' he called, and then to Tony's consternation he dropped the fork as if it had scalded him, and burst into tears. He grabbed the sad bundle from Tony, hugging it to his chest so hard he thought he would hear bones crack any minute.

'Bryn. Oh, Bryn. Where did you find him?' Tears streamed down Tom's face and splashed onto his hands and the dog's coat. 'Oh, Bryn, you daft thing – where you been to?'

'He was up there in the trees,' Tony replied. 'I don't know for how long but he's going to need the vet, I reckon.'

The commotion had brought Mrs Morgan and Lucy

outside, Lucy, as usual, all snot and streaked glasses, Mrs Morgan plump and homely with her hands covered in flour.

In the end they insisted he had a glass of home-made lemonade before he took off for the bus. Mrs Morgan wrapped him up some of her gingerbread and scones to take home.

'I just happened to be up there,' Tony insisted. 'Anyone could have found him.'

As it was he was surprised at the joy he felt just seeing poor old Tom choking through his tears and fussing over his silly dog.

'Oh, Bryn,' he said, shaking his head. 'Dad's right. You've never got what it takes to be a working dog. You're daft as a brush.'

By the time they'd called the vet, Mr Morgan had come in for his mid-morning break and it was all Tony could do to disentangle himself from the whole family and stop them patting him on the back all over again.

Not Lucy though. She was the only one who didn't join in all the excitement and relief at Bryn's return. She sat stony-faced and Tony thought maybe she hadn't missed him at all.

He looked at his watch and knew he'd have to run. He made his excuses and cut into the chat. Mr Morgan got up to let him out and clapped him on the back for the third time.

'Thanks, boy,' he grinned. 'Tom was beside himself over that daft dog.'

Tony got off the bus, not even certain he should be bothering at all. He headed up the main drive of the caravan park until he reached the bend with the overgrown path.

It was all gone. The circle of tatty vans, Margaret's bright trailer and her cheerful garden of gnomes. It was as if none of it had ever been there. Now there was a white paved path with flower beds on either side, and the whole thing looked so settled that he wondered whether he'd got the wrong place.

He hardly noticed the thickset man in overalls who had rolled up on his bike and was giving him a curious stare. 'You lost, son? You should ask at the office there if you're looking for someone.' He pointed back the way Tony'd come.

The office was a low, white building which was quiet apart from one man with a red face complaining about his kettle.

'Now you're not going to give me any trouble, are you?' said the young receptionist with the blonde ponytail when she'd seen off the complainant.

'I wasn't planning to.' Tony smiled back at her.

'What can I do for you then?'

'I came looking for some friends of mine. The Lords. But they've gone.'

She looked at him in surprise. 'Middle of this week. Place is a lot happier without them,' and then she stopped and gave an apologetic wave of the hand. 'I'm sorry. I don't want to be rude about your friends.'

He smiled back. 'Well, they weren't all my friends. Just

Chris really. He's in my school. And I knew his mum. She was nice.'

'That poor lad,' the receptionist said in a whisper. 'They haven't found them you know. Since they took off. Him and his mum.'

CHAPTER TWO

Margaret's Gift

Tony's ears pricked up. 'When was this?'

The receptionist searched through an imaginary diary in her head and brought it to mind. 'Just over a week ago. You remember. After we had the storm and the flash floods?'

Tony nodded.

'Well that's when they ran away. It was really only because of Margaret that Dad let them stay. So it wasn't a difficult decision in the end to get rid of the rest of them.'

'Dad?' Tony asked, puzzled.

'Callum Davies. He's the site manager here. I'm his daughter Holly. Holiday job,' she said with a face that said the sooner it was finished the better.

'You don't know where they went?'

Holly shrugged. 'Back on the road like before, I suppose.'

'You haven't got an address?'

'No idea. Sorry.'

'And no one's seen Chris since?'

'No. Gone like the wind. Dad says he's best out of it and I agree.'

'Well, thanks anyway.'

'It's no problem. Wish they were all as easy as you,' she grinned as Tony turned towards the door. She was already turning back to the desk and the big diary that lay open on it when she was joined by a sharp-faced woman with glasses on a chain who called after Tony: 'Excuse me, but were you asking after the Lords?'

'Yes.'

'What did you say your name was?'

'Tony,' he said. 'Tony Lewis.'

'Yes, that was the name. Margaret had something put by for you. You'd better take it.'

She went across to the pigeonholes where all the mail was kept.

'For me?' Tony said, puzzled. 'From Margaret? When did she leave it?'

'Oh, Friday lunch on the day of the storms. What would that be? More than a week ago.'

Tony knew exactly how long ago it was. 'But,' he frowned, 'I hadn't even met her then.'

Before he knew it he was standing at the bottom of the drive with the parcel in his hands. When he opened it there was an odd-looking doll with red hair and green eyes. It looked a bit like Eleri might if she'd been stretched.

Well, that did it. Margaret really was nuts.

94

Dad wasn't happy that he'd been out all day after being ill but he'd kept him his favourite, shepherd's pie, warmed up from lunch.

Tony was halfway through his food when Dad suddenly slapped the kitchen table. 'I knew there was something I'd meant to tell you. While you had the flu this man phoned and wanted to speak to you. I told him you were ill, but he left his number. I've got it somewhere.'

'Who was it?' Tony asked through a mouthful of mince.

'Said his name was Edwin something. A friend of Margaret's? Anyway the number's up there in the cat.'

The cat was a long sleek-looking letter holder and Tony could only just stop himself from getting up and grabbing the number there and then. He'd lost all interest in his tea. 'Better see what he wants,' he said when he'd helped with the dishes, trying to hide his growing excitement. He punched in the number.

'Edwin Storr,' said a soft Welsh voice he didn't recognise.

'Er hello. You phoned and left a message. My name's Tony Lewis.' And then, thinking that might not be enough, he added, 'A friend of Margaret and Chris.'

'Ah yes.' The voice sounded warmer now and a bit less suspicious. 'The boy with the lovely voice.'

'Er, yeah, something like that. Sorry it's taken so long but I've had flu. I'm sorry, I don't remember you at all.'

'Well, you wouldn't, Tony. We hardly got a chance to meet, you and I, before you made such a mess of things.'

He didn't know what to say to that.

'It was all a bit confusing,' was all he managed in the end.

'I think you'd better come over,' Edwin said.

'When?'

'Why not now? I'm not far and you know the place.'

'I do?'

'Just come to the grove, Tony. I'll meet you there.'

Tony put the phone down. 'Oh, Dad, if it's all right the Morgans said I could go back and see how Bryn was. And then I could also say thank you for the gingerbread.' He felt guilty but knew that Dad would never let him go if he told the truth.

'I shouldn't let you, especially after today. Oh, go on then. But don't be later than seven.'

🌲🌳🌲🌳🌲🌳🌲

The grove felt more familiar this time. The man called Edwin was waiting under the furthest beech, the tree which was a little distant from the rest. Tony saw him as he remembered him, the old man with the white hair and the beak of a nose. The one who'd arrived with the flashy bloke in the bright coat, just before the warriors appeared.

'Hello, Tony,' he smiled. 'I'm Edwin.' Then he stepped out from under an overhanging branch with his hand outstretched. Tony went to grab it and then gasped in shock when he noticed the great black birds watching them from the oak tree.

Not blackbirds, which would have been OK, but a whole load of crows, rooks and grey-headed jackdaws. They sat in solemn, silent rows and every eye seemed to be fixed on Tony and Edwin.

96

Tony shivered. He was used to crows but he didn't like the feel of them watching him like this. He was almost afraid to move.

'We seem to have company,' Edwin said a little too cheerfully.

'Yeah.' Tony accepted Edwin's guiding hand.

'They must be guarding something,' Edwin said. 'Anyway my house is just down there so they needn't trouble us. Are you ready?'

Tony looked at Edwin, and then at the birds, and the bad feeling was growing by the minute. There was something that Edwin wasn't telling him. Whatever it was, he decided, the old man was probably just trying to protect him.

Then he felt it again at the edge of his vision. That feeling somewhere between a rustle and a sweep of black wings.

Just then, a huge shadow passed over him and a bird landed heavily in the oak tree. He looked in wonder at its cruel beak and the tatty ruff at the neck. It was a raven.

The branch had only just recovered when two more birds swept in and settled next to the first. 'Gronk,' they croaked at each other and the middle one flapped its wings, almost as if asking for attention.

'Tony.'

He looked up startled. His name there, like a whisper on the wind.

He looked at Edwin and knew he hadn't heard it.

'Are they?' he asked.

'Ravens, yes,' Edwin replied. 'We'll go then, shall we?'

He set off downwards at a brisk pace with Tony slightly stumbling in his eagerness to follow. He knew it was still a bit early for birds to be preparing to roost. It felt odd and he was only too happy to get away from the place.

Then a further surprise. They were heading towards Eleri's bungalow.

Without warning, an angry bird swept over him and made a direct sweep at Edwin. Tony had to put his hand over his eyes as they both began to run. The same raven swooped and croaked furiously, followed by the others. Tony looked back towards the grove and saw to his astonishment that the rest of the birds had gone. How was that possible?

Not that he had time to give it any further thought because he was trying to fend off the flapping and squawking ravens. 'His agents,' said Edwin. 'And I suppose only to be expected. Foul creatures.'

As if in confirmation, a raven dived straight for Edwin's eyes, while the other two wheeled above him and croaked their encouragement.

CHAPTER THREE

The Seven

'I used to like crows,' Tony muttered, bending down to protect his face.

'Get the door open and when I say so get yourself in. I'll handle these.'

Tony wasn't going to argue and belted up the drive just as the ravens turned on Edwin. Horrified, Tony saw him almost fall under a fresh onslaught of beating wings and furious claws. He froze in that moment of looking back. Something wasn't right about this.

'Run, Tony!' screamed Edwin amidst the scramble of wings and claws.

The key fitted easily into the lock. Tony barely had time to take in the tidy hallway, free of dead takeaways, when he heard a crack like gunshot and a loud squawk which was almost a scream.

A bright flash then and more shrieking. Peering round the door, Tony could see that one of the ravens was down and flapping pathetically on the drive while the other two croaked their distress above it. Suddenly Edwin was with him, red-faced and sweating, one side of his face streaming with blood.

'A timely reminder,' he panted as he ushered Tony into the kitchen. 'As if we needed one.'

Five minutes later, Edwin was looking at him over the top of his mug while the rocking chair creaked back and forth. Tony sat staring at the floor, trying not to remember how the three birds had looked as they'd dived at him. Despite all the commotion, though, it didn't look as if they'd done any harm. There were dabs of blood here and there but little more.

He broke the silence at last. 'I don't even know who you are.'

'Well, my name is Edwin Storr and I was a librarian, before I retired. But I'm also one of the Seven, Tony. Same as you, and as I'm sure you've worked out, the same as your friend Margaret and her lump of a son.'

Tony frowned. Chris was a mate, and he didn't like to hear him referred to like that, but then, he supposed, that's how everyone else – Dizzy Davies, Mr Pryce, even Chris's own father – thought of him.

'Have a biscuit, Tony. See, I've put some ginger snaps out specially.'

Tony snatched eagerly at the biscuits, grateful for the sugar. He'd just about stopped shaking.

'The princess told you what it all means, I expect?'

Tony frowned, trying to remember, and took another bite of the biscuit as if the sugar rush would somehow help. It still felt odd to think of his friend as an ancient Welsh princess.

He remembered what she'd said as they'd sat in this very room on the night of the storm. When everything had been put right and the head was back where it should be, seven people were charged with guarding the cauldron, seven who would wake if anyone threatened to use the cauldron's power.

'Eleri told me some of it,' he said aloud. 'But she never had a chance to explain what it all meant. Where did those warriors come from? Where did they take her? Was she trying to get away from Lord Arran?'

'Ah him,' said Edwin with a grim smile. 'I think you know how dangerous our enemy is by now. And how unwise it would be to cross him further. He has already shown his strength. I saw them take both Margaret and Edwin as well. It must have been on his orders.'

'Er, except that you're here,' Tony chipped in. 'You're Edwin and I'm sitting here eating your biscuits.'

'Of course.' Edwin gave an embarrassed laugh. 'Our recent ordeal must be affecting me. I meant your friend Chris, of course.'

Something else was puzzling Tony. 'But I thought Margaret and Chris had run away. That's what they said at the caravan park.' He realised he had no idea where they had gone at all.

'Well, that is much better news,' Edwin said, carefully avoiding Tony's gaze as he tried to clean the bird mess off his glasses. 'I'm sorry but I can't pretend to you that that last incident hasn't been rather distressing for a man of my years.' He paused and gave Tony a sharp look. Then his face relaxed into a smile. 'Your friend Eleri has told you a little about the Guardians of the Cauldron, and why they were set to guard it?'

Tony nodded, eager for the full story now.

'Well, as the prophecy tells, the Guardians can only be

woken at a time of great danger. When, in other words, the cauldron itself is threatened.

'The Seven are the ones who will, when danger arises, find a way of awakening the Guardians of the Cauldron, to help prevent it being used again.'

Edwin was quite animated now, although his voice had lost its sing-song quality. Tony wondered whether this was his 'librarian's voice'.

'Of course, your poor mother and her talent for painting must have roused the Guardians initially. She would have made a good Seeker. It was seven paintings she created after all, wasn't it?'

'Mm, what? Oh yes, sure,' said Tony, remembering that there had been an eighth picture, but checking himself just in time.

'Tony?' Edwin's voice broke the silence. 'What's wrong?'

'Oh nothing. I said I'd be back before dark. I said I was going to call in at the farm to see how Bryn is. So I suppose I'd better. That's sort of my excuse for coming here.'

'Bryn?' asked Edwin as he settled back down in the rocker again.

'The Morgans' dog,' Tony said. 'Down at the farm. I found him up in the grove earlier. He went up there with Lucy and went missing when she did. He's just come back.'

'What?' Edwin shot up so suddenly, the shocked chair continued rocking at a furious pace. 'I knew nothing about a girl.' His face was suddenly hot and red. 'You say she went missing in the grove. When?'

'Oh, I don't know. Getting on for a couple of weeks ago.' Tony tried to explain.

'Who is she?' Edwin snapped.

'Lucy. Tom Morgan's sister. She kept following Eleri home, and . . .'

'How long was she gone for?'

'Wasn't more than a couple of days. Eleri said she was back by the time of the storm. Why? What's up?'

To Tony's surprise, Edwin had started to usher him out.

'What's the matter? What have I done?'

'Maybe nothing,' Edwin smiled. 'Or else more than you thought.'

'So why do you want me to go now then?'

'Not you, Tony. Both of us. You're going to pay that visit to the Morgans sooner than you expected.'

'Why?'

They were halfway out of the door and Edwin's enthusiasm was becoming annoying. 'Because, Tony, where did she get to?'

'How should I know?' Tony shrugged. 'It was only Lucy Morgan.'

'Which is why we'll need to ask her,' said Edwin.

'Well, good luck with that,' Tony shouted after him.

CHAPTER FOUR

LUCY PLAYS HER GAME AGAIN

Tony struggled to keep up with Edwin down the steep side of the slope. The old man moved easily, sidestepping branches and holes in the earth.

Tom was playing with Bryn in the farmyard when they got there and when Tony checked his watch it still wasn't anywhere near seven.

'Come to see how Bryn's doing,' he said cheerfully. 'And this is Edwin. He wants a word with your Lucy.'

A shadow crossed the cheerful face. 'Good luck to him. Anyone would think she didn't want Bryn back. And she was the one who almost lost him in the first place, mind. Here now, Bryn.'

Tony didn't need to ask where they'd find Lucy because he saw her standing playing with a yo-yo near one of the outbuildings.

'You here again?' she said without enthusiasm.

'Came to see how Bryn was.'

'Well, you can see, can't you? Vet says he was lucky but he's going to be fine. Great daft dog.'

'You were there when he disappeared, weren't you, Lucy?' said Edwin.

She looked sourly at him. 'What's it to you?'

'Mr Storr wants to ask you some questions,' Tony tried

to explain. 'About when you disappeared that time. And about Eleri,' he added.

'Her,' Lucy spat back. 'She's a right big fake she is. I saw right through her. I'm glad she's gone.'

'When did this happen, Lucy?' Edwin pressed her gently. 'This with the dog?' The sing-song kindness was back in his voice.

Lucy looked at him, scowling and continually pinging the yo-yo.

That only seemed to make Edwin smile more. He waited, all patience.

It worked. Lucy stopped in surprise, catching the yo-yo in mid jerk. 'Rest of them won't hear it,' she mumbled and gave one great sniff. 'They say I dreamt it.'

She stamped her foot hard, her face red and upset. 'Didn't make none of it up,' she protested. 'It was my birthday.'

'Tell us, Lucy.' Edwin laid a gentle hand on her left shoulder.

She looked ready to throw it off but then stopped. 'It was that daft dog got me into all this.'

Edwin smiled his encouragement.

'Ran off scared and don't know why I bothered chasing after him. I found him up there, lying down next to one of the trees. You know – that one on the end with the big feet. He wasn't doing any harm so I just left him and went in the middle and did my dancing game.'

'What game is that, Lucy?'

'One I always do. Counting with the seven of them.'

'Show me.'

'Might not remember all of it.'

'A bit of it then.'

Lucy gave one of her loud sniffs. 'Well, it's like one, one-two, one-two-three, one-two-three-four, and stamp on the first "one" each time. But then I started coming out with these words.'

'What words?'

'Oh, I can't remember. Some old stuff about Seven. Like a rhyme it was in my head. But I'd never known it, see.'

Tony's gaze had gone from Lucy's face to Edwin's as he knelt down to her. He was clearly excited as he asked his next question. 'Did anything happen when you said those names, Lucy?'

She nodded eagerly, as if glad finally to have found someone who believed her. 'The tree opened,' she said. 'And I went in. It was weird inside. Like stepping into one of those crazy pictures in that book at school.'

'Which tree was it?'

'The one with the funny hanging branch. The oak tree.'

'And you say you went in?'

'There were these men there, sat round a big table. They were all covered in nasty cobwebs and listening to these two birds singing.'

She was so matter of fact about it that Tony nearly laughed. Tom had stopped playing ball with Bryn now and was ruffling his collar. He was half listening and, Tony thought, maybe beginning to believe her.

'What happened next?' Edwin prompted.

'They said I had to stay.' Lucy's voice was almost a whimper.

'Do you know why?'

'Suppose they were cross with me.'

106

'Why was that?'

'Because . . .'

'Because what, Lucy?' Tony was amazed at how gently Edwin was trying to prise it out of the terrified child.

'Because I opened the door.'

Edwin looked stunned. He clearly hadn't expected this.

'What's wrong?' Tony couldn't help asking.

'Lucy, listen to me,' probed Edwin. 'This was a great big door, wasn't it? Probably had big bolts on it too? And you say you opened it?'

She nodded dumbly.

'And what happened when you did that?'

'There was a big roar like when you hear the sea. And everyone started crying.'

'And what about you?'

She was nearly in tears now. 'Said it was my fault. Dragged me down into one of them chairs and held me there.'

Now she really did burst into tears; great sobs which Tony thought she must have been holding back for a long time. 'It was horrible. One of them just held me, and held me and I thought he – they – were going to kill me, they were so angry. But then . . .'

'What happened?' Edwin's hand was back on her shoulder, concerned, and for the first time Tom was concentrating on someone other than Bryn.

'There was this beautiful music then. And these birds. And I just sort of went to sleep.'

'Lucy listen to me – this is important,' said Edwin, really gently now. 'Now can you remember anything else? You might not even think it's important.'

107

Lucy didn't seem to be so confident any more, and Tony thought how young she looked. She was only little.

Tom was looking as if he couldn't believe any of this. 'You think that's where Bryn got to?' he asked in astonishment. 'Stuck in a tree with a lot of cobwebby old men?'

Edwin ignored him. 'He's only just got out, Lucy, but how were you able to? Can you remember?'

She frowned again. 'I woke up,' she remembered. 'And it was like I heard this voice calling me.' She paused. 'It was lovely,' she said to anyone who would listen. She tilted her dirty face up to Edwin's for a minute. 'Who were they?' she asked. 'Those dusty men?'

'The Guardians of the Cauldron,' Edwin said, and his solemn expression had given way to a sly grin.

'Why are you smiling, Edwin?'

'Because that means it isn't too late. Not too late at all.'

CHAPTER FIVE

The Guardians

They all looked at Edwin for a good minute; his grinning was beginning to get on Tony's nerves.

Tom broke the silence in the end. 'I'd best give Bryn his supper. Needs feeding up he does. Glad you're feeling better, Luce.' He gave her a rather clumsy pat on the back.

'He believes me now,' Lucy sniffed. 'But he won't say nothing to Mam and Dad.'

Tony put into words what he'd been thinking for a while. 'How come Bryn couldn't come back until now? How come he never got out?'

'I have absolutely no idea,' said Edwin. 'Nor why you found him there today. Tell me, Lucy,' he asked, 'would you be scared to go back up there? If you didn't have to go on your own, that is?'

Lucy was looking at her feet, and then at Tony. She gave him an odd look. 'It's all her fault isn't it? Eleri?'

'No, Lucy, it isn't,' said Edwin. 'She's gone too. And we have to get her back.'

Tony almost sighed in relief. It was the thing he hadn't had the chance to ask Edwin in the bungalow.

But Lucy just scowled. 'Don't see why we should. It was 'cos of her I got put in there.'

'And because of her, I rather think, that you were able to get out,' said Edwin impatiently. 'Now are you going to come and try? We'll both be with you. Why don't you just go on ahead?'

Tony didn't like the idea of having Lucy Morgan for company any longer than he had to, but he wanted to get Eleri back and was willing to try anything.

Lucy was leaning against the middle tree in the grove with her hands stuffed in her pockets. It was now quite dark and she blinked under the light of Edwin's torch. 'If you can just remember what you did, Lucy,' he called up to her, 'then we can try and get you to do it again.'

Lucy looked down at them as they heaved themselves up the last few yards. She was sniffing as usual and Tony wondered whether she ever blew her nose. She looked nervous, and there were tear tracks on her face. He started to worry about her parents. Edwin hadn't asked their permission. Tony worried about his own dad too.

'Lucy,' Edwin called again.

She just stared at them and sniffed.

Losing patience, Tony ran up to where she leant against the tree and grabbed hold of her shoulder. 'Didn't you hear what Edwin said?'

'No.' She looked puzzled.

'She's deaf,' said Edwin. 'That's right isn't it, Lucy?'

'Just in my left ear,' she said defiantly. 'Since I was little. You just talked to me on my wrong side.'

It all reminded Tony of something he couldn't quite bring to mind.

'Now, Lucy. Let's see what you can remember.' Edwin widened the torchbeam so they were all standing within it. 'Just do what you did before.'

'But it's dark,' she wailed, then she stood for a few silent seconds longer before beginning her dance.

'One
One-two
One-two-three
One-two-three-four
One-two-three-four-five
One-two-three-four-five-six
One-two-three-four-five-six-SEVEN.'

Lucy stepped and hopped her birthday sequence but she wouldn't have done it if there hadn't been others to keep her safe.

Tony watched her and saw how it changed. One minute she was a little girl playing a familiar game. Then a wind came from nowhere and grabbed hold of her, neither bowling her over nor sweeping her away, but taking her up and picking up the spin that had set her pointing towards the fifth tree, and turning its momentum against her.

Again she spun like a top. She roared around in an exhilarated scream as the wind took her up. She played the game but this time she had no choice and the voice which came from her and the words it spoke were not her own.

'Who will take the Seven home
And bring the Dark Lord from his throne?

> Who will show the Mage the skies
> And bring the Bard an end to lies?
> Who will raise the Ship again
> And free the Princess from her pain?
> Who will teach the Lost to fight
> And bring the Child into the light?'

Between Lucy's stamping, her huge voice and the roaring wind, Tony almost had to block his ears.

Suddenly Edwin screamed: 'Ask after the Seven!'

At which the fifth tree swung open and a gentle voice called out, 'And who will bring them home?'

🌲🌳🌳🌲🌳🌲🌳

The Guardians were seated around the table. They looked old and tired draped in their cobwebs. A tall figure with cropped black hair and grey eyes played softly on a harp but no one seemed to notice. Were the others even awake?

Tony choked back his disappointment that Eleri wasn't there. Why had he ever thought she would be?

'The doors,' said Edwin to him, and as he said it Tony looked across and for the first time noticed the wide-open doors.

To his astonishment Edwin was pushing Lucy roughly forward towards them. Surely he wasn't intending that she should shut them?

Lucy gave one last sniff, and then to Tony's amazement she grabbed hold of the twin doors and strained to pull them back towards her.

'Wait,' Edwin said. 'Not yet.' He beckoned Tony forward. 'We must go through first.'

At that, the harp player rested his instrument against one knee and turned to watch them. 'You have come then?' He seemed to be directing his words at Tony. There was something familiar about his voice too.

The man seemed less interested in Edwin. But at least he didn't look as sad as the rest of the company.

'Lucy,' Edwin called and she went to him like an obedient puppy. This wasn't the Lucy Morgan that Tony knew. 'We will go through and then you must shut the door after us.'

She gave him a look in which fear and uncertainty were battling and she looked a lot smaller.

'There is nothing to be afraid of. This time the outer door will stay open so that you'll be able to go back.'

'But . . .'

'No one will stop you. You made a mistake. You were not to know.'

'Not to know what?' Lucy snapped with some of her old fire.

'Quickly, child. The window between the worlds is only open for a time.'

Whatever that meant, thought Tony. Now it was his turn to feel nervous.

'Do you go in search of . . . ?' It was another of the group who had started to speak. He was tall and gaunt and great seamed scars ran down his right cheek. He scowled under an unruly shock of silver-black hair.

A shorter man patted him on the shoulder. 'No, he seeks another.'

113

Edwin was urging Tony forward. Tony wasn't sure he wanted to go. 'But I said I'd be back by seven,' he protested. There was something odd and rushed about all this that he didn't like. 'Who are they talking about if it isn't Eleri?' he hissed, with an angry shove at Edwin's hand.

'Pah,' Edwin snapped. 'They don't know the difference between waking and sleeping. Pay no attention.'

But Tony sensed their kindness and wisdom. He wasn't sure he wanted to be forced who knew where by some impatient old bloke. And Dad would be getting worried.

'Go through and wait.' The man with the silver-black hair had risen to his feet. He had to be nearly seven feet tall. 'I must talk with the boy alone.'

Tony could see the protest beginning in Edwin's face, but it was cut short by the other's eyes which were as deep and brown as freshly turned earth.

'And we will deal gently with Lucy when you are gone,' the harp player added. 'She meant no harm.'

'It was just a game,' Lucy tried to protest, but Edwin was at her shoulder, steering her back to the side of the great door.

'Can't you do it?' Lucy protested with the tears filling her eyes. 'It was you they were waiting for, wasn't it?'

Edwin looked back at Tony. 'Don't be long or the chance will be lost,' he said and went through the door.

CHAPTER SIX

THE CAVE INTO NOWHERE

The tall man beckoned to Tony. 'There isn't much time,' he said. 'I'm worried. Something doesn't feel right.'

Tony looked at him, instinctively trusting him. The man returned his gaze with a searching intensity.

'I don't even know where I'm going,' Tony began to protest. 'Or what's out there.'

'You will find yourself on the shores of a place called Uffern,' the man with the scars answered. 'It forms the gateway to the underworld of Annwn. Look for the cave.'

Which, as usual, thought Tony, told him everything and nothing. 'Will we find Eleri there?'

The two seemed to exchange an odd glance. There was a pause. 'You may see our sister, Branwen,' the taller man said at last. 'But you have been called by one who needs you more than she does . . .'

'Your sister? Who are you then?'

'Tony?' The impatient call from Edwin interrupted whatever the other had been going to say. 'We are running out of time. Hurry.'

And Tony felt an overwhelming tiredness overtake him at that moment. He'd have liked nothing better than to sink into a chair.

'When you reach the cave you must go into it,' hissed the man with the scars. 'They will tell you how to find him.'

'But find who?' Tony cried in despair and annoyance. 'And what about Eleri? I thought we were going to rescue her.'

'Maybe, but perhaps you should worry less about Eleri.' The man smiled, and Tony saw the humour and kindness behind the scars. 'You'd better go now or you may not go at all.'

'Tony!' roared Edwin till his impatient bellow was cut off by an answering roar from the sea.

Tony headed down through the great hallway. He still could not believe he was inside a tree. He looked back. 'What about Lucy?'

And that was something new as well. Caring what happened to Lucy Morgan.

'We will take care of her,' the harp player called back.

Lucy stood there uncertain for a while.

'Close the door now, Lucy.'

'But,' she said, 'I'm not sure I can. Can't you do it for me . . . ?'

'Only the one who opened it.'

'But what if I . . . ?' Then she shrugged and seemed to remember who she was. She grabbed hold of the doors with all her wiry young strength, and pulled them back towards her. There was a horrible grinding noise, and part of the bottom beam began to split, but she continued pulling as the assembly looked on.

Then with a great deal of complaining effort and creaking from the splintered timber, she shot the bolt across and a huge crash resounded throughout the great hall.

Lucy looked around her. 'Can I go now?'

The answer was unexpected. A rush of birdsong, sweeter than before.

'It has been hard for you, Lucy,' the tall man smiled.

Lucy Morgan hardly heard him. All she wanted was to get home for supper. In her mind she was already scampering out of the tree and panting down the slope and away from the grove.

The tall man put a hand on her shoulder to stay her.

Tony looked in front and behind him. All he could see was golden sand. All he could hear was the building roar of the sea as the tide came in. Where was the cave?

'Where have they gone? Where have you dragged me to anyway?'

Edwin smiled. 'Hardly dragged, Tony. I'm sorry, but I thought you wanted to get your friend back.'

'Yeah but . . .' He stopped himself from asking about what the ancient ones had said about Eleri not needing him as much as someone else did.

'It will soon be dark,' said Edwin. 'I think we should gather some driftwood for a fire. If we can find enough that will burn we can at least keep ourselves warm.'

It made some sort of sense, thought Tony. But then the tide would come in within a few hours and overrun them. 'We need to look for somewhere to shelter,' he said. 'To keep warm. And dry.'

'But if you look at the sky you'll see it's already getting dark,' Edwin replied. 'And I'm responsible for you. I can't have you getting lost, can I?'

He's got a point, Tony thought. It was about the first thing he'd agreed with.

But still it would be a better idea to look for the cave. He made a decision. 'You look for wood on that side of the beach and I'll try this way.'

'That's excellent, Tony,' Edwin smiled and headed off.

Instantly Tony found what he was looking for. How could he have missed it? It was as impossible as most of the other things that had happened in the last couple of days.

The cave was almost at his shoulder and he realised with a thrill that, in some weird way, only he could see it. If Edwin turned back, all he would see was Tony looking for firewood.

He also knew that if he hadn't been told to look for it, then he wouldn't be finding it now. For some reason it was only for him.

With the appearance of the cave the landscape had changed too. He was standing on sand but behind him, leading up to the cave entrance, were piles of boulders and pebbles. Many of the rocks were covered with slimy seaweed. He would need to tread carefully. In his nostrils was the salty reek of the sea.

At the entrance, Tony gave one last, almost guilty, look towards the figure of Edwin, now much further down the beach.

The sun was dipping fiery orange below the horizon.

Tony shivered and turned towards the beckoning darkness of the cave.

Bending his head, he climbed down some irregular steps, careful as he went because one or two were crumbling. The steps wound down onto a wider, deeper sandy floor. The sand was the soft kind you could run through your toes. Without thinking, he took off his shoes and socks and carried them in his left hand, using his right to negotiate whatever was ahead. The sand was warm, almost hot in here.

'Gronk.'

The sound echoed from further back in the cave. There was a brief flutter and for one terrifying moment an image came back to him of swooping and clawing in a cloud of black. Then for some reason he was smiling.

'Gronk.'

All of a sudden the place was full of light. Light that came from thousands of candles. They ranged from simple nightlights to tall beeswax candles that looked as if they might have come from a church. There were squatting red ones and even one or two purple ones belching thick smoke. Some were hanging in the air, or maybe he just couldn't see what was attaching them to the rocks.

'Gronk.'

The whole effect was like a crown of lights and Tony had the oddest sense that it was just above his head. He liked candles but this was all a bit over the top.

'The candles are there for a reason. So that you might see better.'

'Eleri,' he called into the lights, but he knew it wasn't her voice. Instead, ahead of him, he could see a robed figure huddled over a huge cauldron from which steam issued. It smelt of old socks.

'What do I need to see?' he asked nervously.

'In the cauldron, Tony. Your past, your present . . . and your maybe future.'

This was just too much. 'Look, I'm not being funny but . . .'

'There is no time, Tony. You must look.'

CHAPTER SEVEN

THE CAULDRON

This time the voice snapped into him like a leather strap and without warning he was up in the air, jerked forward off his feet until he was hanging there suspended above the candles. On either side of him the three ravens flew and 'gronked'; for some reason their presence filled him with joy.

Or it would have done if he hadn't been so worried about what was holding him up. He felt like some dangling puppet. Was it the birds who were doing this, or maybe the old woman? He felt his stomach lurch and without warning he was dropped tumbling into the heart of the cauldron.

The sandy floor of the cave had been warm. The contents of the cauldron burnt and scorched. He tried to will it all into a dream but he just screamed instead because this was an agony he'd never imagined. It must have lasted no more than a few seconds, but just when he thought he could stand the pain no longer, it began to ease.

'Good,' said the same voice. Which wasn't how it had felt.

The burning was gone and he was in the same place that he'd left, except without the candles. An inner cave in darkness with some kind of agitated fluttering all round him.

'Where am I?' he called.

'In the cauldron,' the same crabbed voice answered. 'You are part of it now and it is part of you.'

'Why?'

'You are being made stronger for what is to come.'

'Yeah, well, if I just knew what that was.'

'Gronk.'

Tony tried to see where the birds had gone. There was another agitated flutter. 'Why did you attack Edwin?'

A cacophony of angry squawking.

'It is time to see the eighth card,' the witch voice said again.

'What eighth card?' he called out into the blackness. 'I can't see a thing.'

'Margaret would have shown it to you if she hadn't been interrupted.'

'I didn't know there was an eighth card.'

'Of course there is. The Alder boy. Did you think you could ignore him?'

'I . . . I . . .' In the end he just gave up. The dark was making him sleepy. 'Whatever. I don't understand any of it. Show me what you like. It won't do me any good.'

There was a brief flare like a match and the image lit up in front of him.

He could see all around him now. The cave had an uneven floor. There were damp walls on either side and a crack high above, through which you could see a patch of dark sky. The grey-veiled old woman bent over her cauldron. Three great birds perched on a rock and eyed him with suspicion.

Their feathers were battered and the ruffs at their necks tatty. Cruel beaks curved and eyes flashed bright intelligence. Each one of them looked as if it could have eaten a couple of crows.

'Gronk,' one of them called.

But Tony hardly noticed. He was looking at the image which had formed on the roof of the cave. A picture that made him shiver, a throned child encased in ice. There was ice on the ground, and climbing the walls of the chamber, but it had coated the boy too. Ice seemed to be eating the seated figure so that only his eyes and the ends of his fingers were visible.

'Who is he? Why is he in that horrible chair?' Pause. 'Why does he look like me? Is this another of Mum's pictures?'

Maybe this was the Alder boy, he thought. There was a similarity. Tony imagined that if he were to find a picture of himself at seven years old it might look a bit like that. It wasn't a nice feeling.

Another flash and to his relief the picture of the ice boy was gone. Just the crouching woman at her cauldron, with the three ravens perched above her. To his astonishment he found that he could understand their gronks now.

'You must go soon,' said one.

'He has sent for them.'

'They are terrible.'

'Who has? And who are *they*?' Tony called out in desperation.

The old woman paused in her stirring and unbent to look up at him. Behind the swirls of grey he saw a pair of piercing bright-blue eyes.

'You must not delay,' she warned him. 'You must go inwards. While there is still time.'

Tony's mind was a whirl of confusion. The scalding-hot cauldron that wasn't a cauldron. The birds whose squawks he could now understand. This old woman. And a cave that wasn't really there.

'The cave will be here when you need it.' The old woman pulled aside her veils to look at him. Her blue eyes seemed to strip away every layer he had. 'You do not remember any of it?' she said, and this time her tone was softer. She shook her head sadly.

'What is there to remember?' Tony shrugged, and wondered why the three birds huddled closer together on their perch.

'Much,' she said. 'But not now. Now you need to act quickly.'

He was becoming impatient. 'Are you going to tell me where to find Eleri?'

'She is not your concern.'

At that, the ravens recommenced their frenzied gronking. Any brief alliance they might have had was over. They were almost fighting.

'Be still,' the old woman commanded them.

As they stopped their squabbling Tony saw that one of them was different from the others.

He had failed to see it at first when they were fluttering above him, but now it was clear. One of the ravens was

124

struggling. One of its wings was, if not broken, then next to useless.

He remembered them from the grove. Could that only have been earlier this evening? Dad would be so worried. He shouldn't have done this.

'Your father will be fine, Tony. He will understand.'

Then Tony remembered the raven struggling on the path leading up to the bungalow, its fellows squawking their distress above it. And Edwin's face streaming with blood after they had attacked him.

And Edwin had not seen the cave like he had. Why? Edwin was building a fire so that he could wait. For what?

'Because he is not Edwin.'

The statement had come from the raven with the damaged wing. It was no longer a raven but a woman. She was tall and pale with long black hair, dressed all in black apart from a golden chain at her neck. Even her eyes were like deep black holes. Tony could see the pain on her face and the way she could not move one arm.

'Who is he then? How?'

'You do not need to know,' replied a second woman and, where the first seemed to fit in with the darkness of the cave, this one blazed with light. Her hair was red and fell past her waist; she wore a dress of red silk. Her eyes flashed green sparkle and mischief.

'Then why has he brought me here?'

If Tony had hoped that this would bring a third transformation he was not disappointed. The first woman was sternly beautiful, the second was younger and mischievous but the third was the gentlest, dressed all in emerald green with golden hair caught up at the back in a golden net. Her eyes were a deep blue. She had a smile that made him ache for his mother.

'So you have decided to show yourselves!' snapped the old woman. 'Why?'

'Surely it is more important to tell the child what to do,' the third woman said with a gentle smile. 'We can squabble at any time after all.'

'He's not Edwin. He's Lord Arran, isn't he?' Tony was trying to ignore everything else. 'Why has he brought me here? What happened to the real Edwin? I knew something wasn't right.'

The old woman interrupted him. 'The boy must go back. He must wait for a rescuer.'

'Excuse me,' said Tony. 'But I am here, you know.'

'But she's right,' said the red-haired woman. 'You must go back and sit by his fire and chit your chat and never reveal what you know.'

'Yeah and why's that?' Tony was getting a bit fed up of having his life organised by strangers.

'Because he might decide to kill you,' snapped the one with the black hair.

'I think I preferred you as ravens,' Tony muttered.

CHAPTER EIGHT

DOLL POWER

As Tony Lewis emerged from the cave, he focused all his concentration on trying to make Edwin believe nothing had changed.

'You managed to find some then?'

Edwin, false Edwin, was smiling at him, adding fresh wood to a fire that was already blazing nicely. The tide was taking its time to come in, so maybe they would have a couple of hours yet. 'I don't know much about it, of course, but Uffern is supposed to be a cave,' he said as he continued to shift bits of wood around to allow the fire to breathe. 'One that leads from our world into . . .' He made an open-handed gesture, 'into wherever we are now.'

'Why's it got such an odd name then? Uffern?' Tony asked innocently and felt a rapid rustle of wings at the edge of his consciousness that felt almost like applause. 'I mean Annwn. Uffern. They're such funny names. What do they mean?'

'Do you really want to know, Tony?'

'Well, I might as well. Looks like we're going to be here a while.'

Edwin laughed. 'Well, if you want to listen to the ramblings of an old librarian . . .'

'Yeah, but I need to know this Welsh stuff. The *Mabinogi* and that.'

'Very well, Tony. Why don't you just continue feeding the fire as we talk? Don't put too much on or you'll choke it. There's an art in fire making.'

'Dad's good at it.'

'In some of the old stories making a fire was a sort of initiation test.'

'So what are you planning to initiate me for then?'

Feeling bold now. Maybe too cheeky?

'Well, I'm not entirely sure that I am.'

'Yeah, but we must be waiting for something. What?'

Tony saw a look pass briefly over Edwin's face. He'd have missed it if he hadn't been looking for it. Then, from nowhere, he saw a flash. It was as if someone was sending a signal. So he had guessed right then. 'Anyway you were going to tell me about those words.'

Edwin frowned before he remembered. 'Well now, most people believe that Annwn means "the deep". Which is I suppose an appropriate description of what we might call an underworld. As for Uffern, well I'm afraid that's a different matter.'

'Why's that then?'

'Because "hell" is the best translation anyone has come up with so far.'

Tony paused in resting two sticks of wood against each other. The birds did their fluttering thing again and it was beginning to get on his nerves. It was like having someone awarding him points.

'Well, it's not exactly hot, is it? I mean we had to make our own fire.'

128

There came another flash. Tony was becoming more and more sure.

'Just a few more pieces now, Tony. That should do it.'

As Edwin turned his head to sort out new bits in the main wood pile, Tony looked behind him to the cave. He wasn't sure what made him do it, perhaps Edwin getting him to do useless things like making a fire they would never use.

The next flash came from in front of them, and some way to the west.

From the cave entrance someone tall was beckoning to Tony. It had to be one of the three women he had met earlier. He had to find out. 'Just need to stretch my legs,' he told Edwin.

The old man was preoccupied. 'Fine.'

🌲🌴🌳🌲🌳🌴🌴

'Tony?' The woman threw back her hood.

He started at his name and would have shouted out if she hadn't shushed him furiously. 'Eleri?'

It was her, only older.

'He is not what he seems.'

'Yeah, guessed that. Signalling to someone. But where did you get to? I thought you were dead.'

'But I sent a message. Margaret . . .'

'Yeah, but she's nuts, isn't she? Anyway you're like Eleri but you're not her. You remind me of my mum.'

The woman squeezed his hand so fiercely he yelped. 'Listen, we don't have much time. They will be here within minutes and they will take you, and me if they find me. Do you still have the doll?'

129

'Yeah, I've got it in my bag. Makes me feel daft.'

'Take it and throw it on the fire.'

Tony looked at Eleri as if she were mad.

'What? Why?'

'Just do it. Don't ask questions,' she snapped.

'All right. Keep your hair on,' he sulked, and wondered why she was grinning.

Tony stumped the few yards back to the fire and Edwin, who wasn't Edwin.

He was bending over the blazing fire, poking at it with a stick. There was another flash to the left, much closer now. 'Enjoy your stroll?' Edwin gave his most pleasant smile.

'It was great. I've found something else to chuck on the fire.'

'Good,' Edwin shrugged. 'What?'

'This,' Tony grinned, pulling the doll out of his bag and throwing it into the blaze.

Edwin's relaxed grin disappeared and he was shouting in fury and terror. 'No. No. How did you . . . ?'

A great furious figure with blazing red hair came roaring up out of the fire. It held something which spat and almost sang. Something made of the finest material, a net of gold so fine but so strong that Edwin could do nothing to resist it. And then he screamed. A horrible scream. He was struggling against the net and all but tumbled into the fire.

Tony could see other familiar features swimming into Edwin's face. 'What is it?' he called back to Eleri in horror. 'What have you done?'

'Run, Tony,' she shrieked as she held up the staff in front of her. 'Run. They're coming.'

As Tony dived for safety within the cave, warriors broke cover from their position behind the rocks and stamped into the place where the signal fire had been set.

CHAPTER OⅡE

LUCY'S PROMISE

'You know her then? The silver lady?'

Lucy had been about to go home and glad about it. Not just because of the dark but because of everything else. She couldn't quite get her head around it, but she was beginning to remember things which all the other worries had covered up.

The man smiled. And he was tall, thought Lucy, and in need of a wash and other things. Normally if some weird bloke had started asking her a load of questions she'd be thinking about yelling or something, but this one was all right.

'So that's how it happened,' he said. 'You met the lady. I should have known.'

'Taught me that rhyme, she did. But the wind keeps taking me and changing the words.'

The tall man leant down to her and took one small hand in his great one. 'Lucy, you must forgive me. All of us. I should have guessed that you hadn't just blundered in by accident. I think it was because of what you did with the door. I'm afraid we were not really ready for visitors.'

''S all right,' she sniffed, not quite convinced.

'Now I realise that you should have been with us all along. You must come back and visit us. After all, you were meant to.'

Lucy wasn't sure. 'Why's that then? Is it something to do with Tony Lewis and that old bloke? You don't like him much, do you?'

The tall man gave her a rueful smile. 'Well, let us say I don't entirely trust him.'

'I don't like him,' chipped in Lucy. 'Keeps coming and going. Is he going to hurt Tony?'

The man let go of her hand and stood up straight. It seemed to take a long time. 'I hope not. There are people on the other side looking out for him.'

'That Eleri. She's one of you, isn't she?' Lucy insisted. 'I knew there was something wrong about her, see.'

'She's one of the ones he can trust, Lucy. And he's got more to him than anyone thinks. Now tell me what the silver lady said to you?'

Lucy scowled in concentration. 'I thought it was a dream for ages after,' she said. 'Where did the rhyme come from? Why did I need to go and do it every birthday? And who's the lady?'

'You liked her?'

'Thought she was a bit funny but, y'know, nice. Now I'm not sure what she was.'

'And she didn't tell you anything else?' The tall man took her hand again and squeezed it gently. 'Not even something you remember from a dream?'

Lucy frowned so hard she had to put her hand to her head with the pain.

'It's all right,' he said. 'It doesn't matter.'

'It was what she didn't say,' she said in sudden realisation. 'Mam and Dad were calling me to see where I'd got to, see. Then she was gone and I never had the chance to ask her. Was it important?'

He didn't answer.

Lucy continued: 'I was just so sad after that. Everyone said I'd changed. And that was when I went deaf.' She touched her left ear, wincing.

The tall man pulled her to him in a clumsy hug. 'I'm sorry, Lucy,' he said. 'It must have been really scary for you.'

Lucy looked at him in surprise. 'Can I go home now?' she said.

'Of course,' he smiled, but sadly. Lucy found herself liking him.

'Are you going to tell me your name?'

'It's Efnisien, I'm afraid,' he replied, the smile fading from his face. 'Now off you go.'

🌲🌲🌲🌲🌲🌲🌲

Tony was taking his time getting used to the new version of his friend. She was taller and more grown-up, yes, but the red hair and the mischievous sparkle in her green eyes were more like the Eleri he remembered.

'So what do we do next?' He had been expecting them to drop back down into darkness. Maybe even to meet the raven ladies and the old witch at the cauldron again, but really it was as if he'd stayed where he was. Only here the shore was sand instead of rocks and the tide was so far out it was never going to be a problem.

'Why didn't those warriors come after us?' he asked as they stood on the top of the dune looking out to sea. 'They were the same ones, weren't they? The ones who took you? You never told me how you got away.'

The green eyes were serious as they looked back at him. 'That is really a story for another time, Tony,' she said. 'But can we just say I was able to make a bargain with them? The sort that they could understand.'

Tony nodded, understanding nothing. Just for a change. 'Will Lucy be safe?' he asked instead. 'I mean with those men? Two of them seemed to be all right. It was weird, though, because the tall one said something odd about you being his sister.'

'There's nothing weird about it,' Eleri smiled. 'He's my brother.'

'What, that big bloke with the scars? Cool.' Tony was impressed.

'I'm glad you liked him.'

'So who was the other one then?'

'Tony, would you mind? I need to concentrate. There's something I'm sort of expecting to be here and it isn't. So I just need to concentrate to work out where it is.'

'What about that fire demon thing and the doll? Is Edwin – Lord Arran, I mean – going to come after us?'

'Certain questions I'm just not able to answer.'

'Because you don't know?'

She looked awkward. 'More like I just can't.'

135

'Typical grown-up,' Tony grumbled. 'Why couldn't you just stay as Eleri? Feels weird like this.'

'Just let me think,' she snapped at him, looking out to sea. 'Oh no!'

'What's up?' But he could see something had changed.

The sea which had been blue and placid had become grey and churning and the gulls and terns were screeching as if they expected something bad. Across the wide expanse of water, Tony could see a ship with an old-fashioned sail being thrown about in the lashing waves. He could just make out the silhouette of a great tower on a shore which seemed an impossibly long way away. It hadn't been there before.

'What is it?'

The wind began to build and buffet them as they stood there on the edge of the dune with the sand driving into them. Eleri looked at him. 'Watch. You need to see this. Although,' she muttered half to herself, 'I wish you didn't.'

Tony was silent as his attention turned to the sailing ship, now struggling across the expanse of grey. The waters were disturbed and suddenly something huge broke the surface. He could see the dots of the men on board but could only imagine their terrified shouting.

'What is it . . . ?' His question tailed away as he looked on in new horror. A huge coiled serpent boiled out of the water and fell upon the ship and its hapless mariners, smashing it to matchwood in a few seconds and then tossing itself around so that they could fall more easily down into its waiting mouth.

'Nothing,' Eleri muttered, white-faced. 'We can do nothing.'

'What's that big tower?' Tony could only just force the words out. He tried not to look at what was happening on the ship but couldn't help himself. The monster fell on the last of the tiny black sticks and then disappeared beneath the waves. From where they stood, the whole thing was soundless.

Soon, only the water showed any signs of disturbance. There were a few smashed sticks on the surface and nothing more. Tony stared out for a long while. Into space and silence.

'In Caer Siddi was Gwern imprisoned.'

The new voice came from somewhere nearby but Tony couldn't see anyone. To his surprise, Eleri was smiling her relief. She addressed the newcomer. 'You're here,' she said. 'I was beginning to think you weren't coming.'

Tony looked at her. Was she mad? Who was she talking to? Where?

'I think it's about time we showed him,' said the voice. Tony felt the pressure of an unseen palm on his forehead and without warning they were somewhere else entirely.

He scarcely had time to adjust before having to dodge a huge wooden platter. A red- and greasy-faced servant was sweeping in with a huge tray of whole roast chickens.

They were in the midst of a magnificent banqueting hall. It was full of bustle and shouting and the sound of meat being torn, and wine and ale being noisily swallowed. Yet more food was being deposited onto a series of wooden tables. Men and women were dressed in the brightest colours. They were mostly young, with hair that was either blonde or nut brown. There was only the odd fleck of grey. This was a place of youth.

On a raised gallery, minstrels played harps and a sort of wooden pipe with a reed. In front of them was a lute player with a sharp nose, and below, on the rush-covered floor in the centre, a fool in jangling bells capered and made faces, trying to distract two jugglers who spun plates and clubs without missing a pass.

Picking herself up, Eleri looked at Tony. He was gazing open-mouthed. She couldn't help smiling.

No one could see them, of course, because none of it was real.

CHAPTER TWO

THE BARD'S TALE

The act was coming to its climax. Only now was it clear how much had been planned. Having intruded further and further into the act, the fool prepared for his final fling. And fling was a good word for it because just as the twin jugglers got the goblets and plates spinning between them in an endless stream, he launched himself at them.

There was a gasp from the huge audience.

He shouldn't have been able to do it, but he did, flipping backwards over and between them, shaving the flying bowls and goblets by inches, only to land on his feet as nimbly as an Olympic gymnast.

The moment he landed, there was an enormous roar and the two jugglers let their equipment drop with a crash and were suddenly pounding him on the back.

When you looked at them together like that, thought Tony, you could see the family resemblance.

He didn't have long to think about it. A chair was being scraped back noisily and a man stood up and clapped his hands; one clap was all he needed to show his authority. He was of medium height with hair and beard of a soft chestnut brown. Brown eyes twinkled and his mouth was clearly used to laughter. Unlike nearly everybody else, he was dressed in dull brown and grey and the only thing which might have made him stand out, apart from the simple gold band on his head, was the great sword strapped to his side.

'It's him,' Tony whispered across from the corner where he'd taken refuge. Eleri was still half hiding under the table and she straightened as everyone's attention turned to the figure who had risen to his feet.

'You're right,' she called. 'It's Arthur.'

'I didn't mean that,' Tony shot back. 'I mean it's him. The one who hit you with his sword. That night in the grove. And I'll bet that's the sword. It must have stung. But how could they have got here so quickly? They were chasing us.'

Eleri didn't say anything. As mesmerised by the man and the scene as Tony was.

'So what happened to him?' Tony insisted.

Eleri didn't answer.

'And they sailed with such hope,' the voice came again from nowhere.

Tony looked in puzzlement for the person who had spoken but could see no one.

'My friends. Brave gentlemen and ladies. Honoured guests and most valued entertainers.' There was a hush around the young king as he addressed the hall. 'I believe tonight I have seen a new definition of brotherhood. For what better example than one which brings the brothers as close together as they dare?'

There was laughter at that.

'A purse of gold for the gallant tumblers.'

A roar of approval.

'Had it gone awry by a hair's breadth it would have been vinegar and paper.'

At which the tumbler himself gave a rueful grin and then a showy bow. Again the crowded hall roared its approval.

'And yet there is a newcomer in our midst. A bard who has not yet chanted.'

A mixed murmuring now.

'But he will sing soon . . .'

Everyone was now filling and raising their cups with the king at their head.

'And by the end of his song . . .' smiled the king.

'. . . he will know the starry wisdom,' Tony muttered, just before everyone else roared the last line like a football crowd.

Arthur waved his hand up to the gallery and, to a ripple of harp song, a figure began to make his way down.

'And this,' the unknown voice said a little more loudly, 'is where it all started to go wrong.'

It was only then that Tony saw the white-bearded figure leaning on his staff and grinning at them.

Tony was torn between the two figures: the one sweeping majestically down the staircase with his jewelled harp and cloak of bird feathers, and the older man with the staff, bending his head to get under the low entrance.

The great bard was speaking now to a buzz of enthusiasm from his audience.

'I will set out on foot,
To the gate I will come,
I will enter the hall,
My song I will sing,
My verse I will proclaim,
And the king's bards I will cast down.'

'And I believe that's quite enough of that,' said the white-bearded man grumpily. 'Taliesin was always in need of an "off" switch, and the king was always too slow to use it.'

Tony was tempted to say 'shh' as if someone was eating popcorn in the cinema but Eleri's face lit up with delight.

'Don't worry,' the man said. 'They can't see or hear me and if they could, this whole disaster might have been avoided. Oh and, yes, you're right – no one can see you. It was most amusing watching you trying to sidestep people.'

Eleri's face split in a huge grin and the old man winked at her.

'You're Merlin.' It was Tony's turn to grin.

'I am. You've rather caught me out there, I'm afraid.'

'No one said you were like this,' Tony frowned.

'Like what, pray?' the other puffed rather haughtily.

'Well, a bit sort of . . . weird,' Tony continued.

'My dear young man, I positively invented weird. Before me it wasn't even on the map. If you're really unlucky you might hear Taliesin sing a praise poem in my honour. You'll be asleep by halfway through though, I guarantee.'

'Cool,' said Tony.

'Except that it's not going to happen. In a few minutes, when he's finished puffing himself up, he's going to tell a story which will change the world.

'And in a bad way,' he added more quietly.

There was a sudden roar of approval as Taliesin finished his great poem with a flourish. It was as if Merlin had turned the volume back up again.

'What though?' asked Tony, puzzled. 'What is he going to do?'

Merlin fixed piercing blue eyes on him. 'He is about to tell the tale which will lead Arthur to his doom. The tale of the great cauldron of Annwn.'

'The cauldron,' whispered Tony, still unable to believe that they couldn't be seen or heard.

'A tale which I have no wish to hear again,' said Merlin. 'In fact I think it is about time I showed you into my *esplumoir*.'

'Your what?' blurted Tony, unable to help himself.

'Why did you bring us here?' asked Eleri.

Merlin looked at them with a scowl. 'You're mistaken if you think I've got anything to do with it. I've only just got back myself. Barely had time to unpack. So if you think I've got the time to . . .'

But Tony saw the twinkle in his eye, and interrupted him. 'They're the same people, aren't they? The same as the ones in the boat who got taken by the dragon or whatever it was. It's the same story.'

Merlin looked at him admiringly. 'They are. You are right. And they have to repeat it time and time again.'

'But why?' Tony asked, puzzled.

'Because that was part of the deal. What's more, even

143

though he was allowed to escape, he has to do it with them. That idiot pupil of mine. And the only clue to the truth is in his cack-handed poem. But the language is so flowery, no one gives it houseroom. Now that's what I call irony.'

'And that's what I call not being able to understand a word you're saying,' Tony said rudely. 'Just when I thought I was getting somewhere.'

'No point soft-soaping you, is there?' Merlin came back. 'If you can't pee, you might as well get off the pot.'

'Yeah, and didn't you know it's rude to listen in on people's thoughts?'

'And why do you imagine I do it?'

'Has anyone ever told you you're just a grumpy old git?'

'More times than I care to count. And because I'm the original grumpy old git, I couldn't give a —'

'Merlin!' scolded Eleri. 'Stop playing with him. Come on!'

She was first through the door onto a wide sandy beach. The murmur and dream of the court was soon behind them. To their right, a rocky path cut deep into the headland and this was where Merlin was striding. It was all Tony could do to keep up with him.

Eleri grinned at his struggle and hung back a bit. 'Have a guess where we're going?'

'How should I know!' Tony grumbled.

'Where else but Merlin's cave. Look.'

CHAPTER THREE

MERLIN'S CAVE

Of course Tony was going to follow, whatever mood he was in. He was too intrigued not to, and he trusted Eleri even if he wasn't sure yet about Merlin. But wasn't this all a bit too, well, convenient? But then, ever since they'd got here, things had been appearing and disappearing without warning. Who was he to argue?

'It may look convenient to you, young man, but I can assure you it isn't at all so to me. Time and time again I have to impart my wisdom to those who show no interest, and do you think I enjoy it?

'And if that's grumpy then maybe it's because I don't much like the world going to hell in a handbag the moment I leave it.'

'What's he chuntering about now?' Tony whispered fiercely to Eleri as they were forced to dip their heads to enter a cave.

'Mind your head now,' Merlin called back, just a bit too late.

'Ow. Ouch.'

'Told you.'

'Ow, you rotten . . .' Tony said ruefully while he rubbed what was going to be quite a bump on the back of his head. He whispered to Eleri. 'He did that on purpose.'

145

'Typical,' Eleri grinned back at him.

'My reputation precedes me, young man. Ah, here we are. Grab a seat – or something that will serve for one. There's only one proper seat, I'm afraid, and I rather think it has the letter "M" on it.'

The last thing Tony expected in Merlin's cave was an office with a smart-looking laptop. He grinned and dragged a broken crate along the floor, trying not to think about the splinters.

'Mind the carpet, will you? It's Axminster.'

'Why are we sitting in front of a computer?' Tony asked, having dragged up his crate.

'Oh, just leave it,' Merlin snapped as Tony tried to pull the carpet out from underneath.

Tony gave up the struggle and perched there with a scowl.

'Where did you go to,' Eleri asked Merlin, 'for all that time?'

'To my *esplumoir.* Which, believe me, my dear, sounds more impressive than it is. If you'd been obliged to stand at the top of an open tower for thousands of years searching for lost patterns in the stars then I dare say you'd be grumpy. Especially if when you found them there was no one left alive to tell.'

'I heard some witch called Nimue had you imprisoned in a rock,' blurted Tony.

'Which was very unfair on her as it turns out. She might have locked me in her chamber and benefited from my charm and charisma,' twinkled the white-bearded rogue, and winked. 'Now just let me concentrate on this for a minute and we can get on.'

There was silence for a second, then a sudden burst of trumpets and a crash of cymbals. Merlin struggled to keep his grip on what looked suspiciously like a joystick. 'Ah, well, you see the funny thing is,' he shouted.

'Watch out!' Tony shrieked, all but startling Eleri from her seat. 'Incoming.'

Merlin did a clever little manoeuvre and just avoided the payload of bombs. It had taken Tony only a few minutes to realise that Merlin wasn't so much playing games with them, as with himself.

There was some banshee shrieking, a hail of swearing from Merlin and then a sign flashed up on the screen.

Game Over.
Your score is 3,985.
You have not made the leader board.
Better luck next time.

'Arse,' said Merlin. 'Now where was I?'

'You hadn't started yet,' scolded Eleri.

'That wasn't anything to do with it, was it?' Tony asked him rudely.

'Never said it was,' Merlin replied. 'It's just that I get itchy fingers if I don't play for a while. And I couldn't be bothered to listen to all that poetry before we got to the main event.'

Then the tension broke and Tony burst out laughing. 'You're just weird,' he howled.

'The weirdest.' Merlin gave a boyish grin. 'Time we were heading back. Mr Wonderful will have coughed up most of that phlegm by now.'

This time he had only to snap his fingers and they were back in the great hall, but now they were looking down from the minstrel's gallery into the hubbub of furious sound below. It didn't help that Tony had rematerialised onto a bench that was already occupied by one of the lute players. He leapt up with a cry of alarm and cursed Merlin.

The young king was now blushing scarlet with rage, and it didn't take Tony long to realise that it was directed at the figure who had previously been the darling of them all, the great bard Taliesin.

'I tell you that if it was anyone other than you, Taliesin, I would have run you through where you stood and then had your head put outside the gates on a spike. A great mouth that speaks too freely loses its worth.'

'And I would gladly submit to the crows and all their ilk, my king, if it would stop the idiocy you are proposing.'

'What idiocy?' Tony whispered furiously.

'Oh, just guess.' Merlin rolled his eyes.

'Are you testing me, bard?'

'Have you ever had reason, my lord, to question either my sense or my loyalty?'

'Not yet,' replied the king dangerously and, reaching down onto the upset table, grabbed hold of his ale cup and drained it dry. 'There is always a first time.'

'Nor should you ever need to,' the bard continued smoothly, ignoring the other's sarcasm. 'You have always honoured my advice before. Why not now?'

Tony saw that the king no longer seemed as young and that there was a shake to the hand which held the cup. 'You go too far.'

'No, my lord,' Taliesin said softly. 'I do not go far enough. What you are suggesting is foolish.'

Uproar again and in the midst of it a burly red-bearded man in chain mail drew a huge sword and leapt towards the quiet figure with the harp.

A hand from Arthur was only just in time to stop him.

'Gwalchmai,' said Merlin, 'sometimes known as Gawain. Nephew to the king and just as hot-headed. Like so many he's not much of a fan of Taliesin.'

Gwalchmai paused before launching the sword at the bard's throat. 'You should let me kill him, my lord. This useless scatter-tongue has insulted you and this realm once too often. Have you forgotten the praise poem?' The words sounded bitter in his throat.

'Every word is etched, nephew, and he was given a whipping for it if you remember. But before I decide to have him put to death I would know what makes him take such a risk in repeating the blunder. Well, bard, have you nothing further to say for yourself? Has your silver tongue quite deserted you? Perhaps I should have it dragged out of you and leave it hanging from my belt as a keepsake.'

Eleri winced at that, as if at the memory of an old wound, but Tony suddenly gasped and turned almost in accusation to Merlin.

The old man was leaning almost nonchalantly, like someone who has initiated a fight and is now trying to weigh up which side to support.

'They're – they're different,' Tony said with horror creeping into his voice. 'More like the men from the grove.'

'They have lost their glamour,' Merlin said simply.

CHAPTER FOUR

THE DUNGEONS OF THE LOST

Tony looked again at the figures who had seemed so golden and youthful. Now the king had food in his beard and dabs of wine decorating his tunic. His face seemed much older, fleshy, and there was a scar on his right cheek which Tony didn't remember seeing before. The rest of the warriors were seated around the wooden benches; they looked more men of violence than of peace, with the red-bearded giant, Gwalchmai, the biggest thug of the lot.

Taliesin didn't seem to belong in that company. His green eyes showed a mixture of rage and sadness. His magnificent cape of birds' feathers and his well-groomed silver-black hair contrasted with the lank locks and grease-stained features of the others.

'But why?' Tony hissed.

'This is how they really were,' was all Merlin would say. 'But the strength of the old magic is very powerful, I fear.'

Tony was only half listening to this because the dangerous argument between king and bard had restarted.

'And pray tell me, my lord, will you carry on with this foolishness despite my advice?' Taliesin waved a weary hand at the swords which had been drawn instantly at this latest insult.

'No one shall stop me taking what is rightfully mine,' roared the king.

'Ah, so now you claim possession!' The bard no longer seemed to care what he said.

'All that lies inside these lands is mine by right, and outside too. This cauldron should not be in the keeping of the lord of the dark lands. It has qualities I need. I will take it, Taliesin.'

'In which case, my lord, it would be foolish to put an end to my life and give the crows and ravens a free meal. Someone must go with you on this fool's errand, someone who knows the nature of the threat. Me.'

Tony saw the relief then in the king's eyes. Perhaps his blustering had been hiding real anxiety; maybe he valued Taliesin more than he made out.

'They will make friends now,' said Merlin. 'And it will be all maps and charts and planning for three weeks until they set out. There is nothing to see now. Come! Time for us to move on.'

'Where to?'

'Where no roads lead and all of them at the same time,' Merlin answered. 'To the dungeons of the lost. To find the prisoner.'

Eleri gave a great shudder as if something nasty was crawling on her neck. Tony looked at her.

Merlin led them and they followed.

To get to wherever they were going, they first had to pass through some kind of underground crypt which made Tony nervous. What if something jumped out at them, all dust and bones and coffin smell?

Without warning, the crypt widened until Tony could

151

see windows which opened onto the sea itself; they were journeying under it. That gave him a strange thrill, so he tried to crane his neck over Merlin's head to get a better look.

On either side were great tombs, many with statues and several with cracked or broken lids. One tomb stood alone on a raised platform, the once-rich carpet beneath it now in shreds.

It looked more cared-for than the others. Meadow flowers decorated the sides, and at its head was a crown wreathed in daisies.

'The White Weaver,' Merlin said, and then to Tony's astonishment, he knelt and reverently placed his hands on the tomb.

'Who is buried here?' asked Tony, as Eleri used her hand to help Merlin up.

'All of those who stayed,' snapped Merlin as he strode forward. 'Come. This is not a place to linger.'

Tony was about to ask what he meant when they were plunged into darkness, and for those few seconds he felt the old childhood thrill in Dan Yr Ogof when the lights went out so that everyone could see what it would be like to live like that.

Just a few seconds and then an eerie light hissed blue into life, and a foul smell drifted over them.

'We are beneath the sea itself.' Merlin's voice was a sonorous clang in the confines of that narrow tunnel. 'Few have, or would wish, to pass where we are going now. This kindle light I can maintain only for a while and you will have noticed that it doesn't smell very pleasant.

'Put your hand to my shoulder as we go, Tony, and you

the same, princess. If, as I suspect, the light doesn't last, then you'll have only my dim memory of these tunnels to guide us back.'

All of a sudden, Tony had a rush of questions. 'How come I can trust you? What makes you different from Lord Arran? Where are you taking us anyway?'

'We are going in search of the one person who can help you,' Merlin called back over his shoulder as Tony felt the slimy walls squeezing and dripping on both sides and tried not to think about what he was treading on.

'Who?' he asked in a hollow kind of voice. 'Why?' Knowing he was beginning to sound like a small child.

'Someone important,' Merlin replied with a tired sort of sigh. 'We are here to find him. He is the one who summoned you.'

'He did?' Tony said before he remembered it was true. That night in the grove. *Then will you help me? Please?* the little voice had pleaded. And then it had asked him to sing. So that's why I'm here, thought Tony to himself. It felt sort of right, although he wasn't sure where the singing came in.

For a while, Tony could only hear Merlin's breathing as they trudged slowly, shoulder to shoulder.

'The prophecy speaks of bringing the child into the light.' Merlin paused. 'And that is the child we go to seek.'

Tony all but tripped over his feet as he tried to make sense of that. 'But I don't know any prophecy,' he stumbled, feeling useless as usual. 'And why does this kid want me to rescue him? He's never met me.'

Confusion was making him agitated and he wasn't

looking what he was doing. This was no place to lose concentration, but that had nothing to do with what happened next. Suddenly he felt himself being jerked backwards and pulled down hard. There was the sound of a curse which must have been Merlin, and a high-pitched scream which had to be Eleri, and then he landed with a crash and everything went black.

🌲🌲🌲🌲🌲🌲🌲

He had no idea how much later it was when he woke up. There was a horrible pain in the back of his head, his neck felt as if someone had wrenched it round, and he felt sick and dizzy all at the same time.

He tried to get up, only to crack his head on a sharp overhang of rock, and tumble back down onto the rocky floor. This time he really was sick and had no idea where it went because it was too dark to see. Then a second and third time; now he was scared. Scared in a new way because he was petrified of the black darkness and had lost the only guide he had in this terrifying place. He could smell the sick on his clothes: it was almost enough to make him gag, but he didn't care.

Finally, exhausted, he slept.

CHAPTER FÍVE

THE PRISONER

When he opened his eyes the pain from his head was easing. In the dim light, he could see that the sick had gone all down his T-shirt and some of it on to his chinos. He got up carefully, looking and feeling like a tramp. Once his eyes adjusted, he saw his surroundings a little better. It was a bit like the cave of the ravens but here, instead of candles, there were tall stalactites and fat bulbous stalagmites. It felt like being in a cathedral. For a few seconds he stood there, open-mouthed, but there was a passage channelling down through the rock and, despite the darkness, he knew he had to follow it.

That was when he heard the crying.

Tony had never done much crying himself, even when his mum had died. Not that this was exactly crying either, more a sort of wailing song, but it was doing his head in. It reminded him of Sophie, when she cried for Mum, and the sound of that made him want to thump his head against the wall.

'Where are you?' he called. Without Merlin and his smelly light and only the faintest gleam from the stalactites, he could hardly see a thing.

The singing just continued. It was eerie and strange. Mum had once told him about the banshee, the wailing

155

Irish spirit which announces a death; it sounded a bit too much like that for comfort.

But with the thin light that came from behind him, Tony peered into the darkness ahead. He felt a new cold close around him and shivered. The wailing continued, above the constant drip, drip down the stone walls, and now he just wanted to block up his ears.

He stopped. The small voice in his head was growing stronger. 'Are you here? Are you coming?'

'Just a minute, will you?' Tony barked, knowing it wouldn't help. Then he cursed and tripped over the laces of his trainers. As he hit the ground again, he realised that the eerie song was coming from beneath him, together with a strange new orangey light, which glimmered up through the cracks. He dropped down. He could clearly hear the sound of breathing below him. It sounded sharp and desperate like someone gasping for air.

'Is he here too? Have you brought him with you?'

'Brought who?' he spoke into the stone.

'My father.' The glow grew warmer as the voice brightened in hope.

'No, sorry. There's only me.'

Tony could almost feel the sigh seep up through the stone. A silence followed as he looked for an entrance that wasn't there.

'Then you must be him. You must be. The one who is to come.'

Oh, here we go again, Tony thought. Whatever.

'You will save me.'

Tony stamped down hard on the stone and heard the ringing clang from underneath him. The voice squealed in excitement. It was beginning to get on his nerves. Then there was that flutter of wings at the edge of sight, and something dark passed behind him.

'If you want to help,' he said in irritation, 'you can just come right out and do it.'

Instead, the singing grew in volume, more like some great chorus on one of Dad's CDs. It was accompanied by a great wave of warmth, and he felt a tingle in every part of him.

'Only you can find the way in,' the eager voice continued from below. 'Only you can rescue me.'

'Guess I've drawn the short straw again,' muttered Tony, fast losing enthusiasm for the rescue. He couldn't work out whether the great choir was connected with the voice. Then as he tried to make out the words he became aware of a deeper note. It was cutting a way through the stream of voices like a sword through wheat.

'Ask after the Seven,' it boomed.

At that moment, Tony realised the confusion of voices was in his own head as much as beneath him, and some part of the song at least was coming out of his own mouth. Just like those times in the grove, he had no idea how he made such a noise.

'The prophecy, Tony,' the voice boomed again.

'I don't know any bloody prophecy.' Tony roared his frustration into the stone floor. Which, of course, was when the words came to him:

> 'Who will take the Seven home
> And bring the Dark Lord from his throne?
> Who will show the Mage the skies

And bring the Bard an end to lies?
Who will raise the Ship again
And free the Princess from her pain?
Who will teach the Lost to fight
And bring the Child into the light?'

On that last line the stone floor cracked beneath him and a blinding blaze of light shot upwards. One minute he was on shaky footing, trying not to tumble down into the cracks beneath, and the next he had steadied himself, the voices in his head and the song pouring upwards in one glorious stream.

'He has come. He has come,' said a delighted voice, and Tony could hear someone clapping his hands with joy.

He steadied himself on a shifting rock and then carefully lowered himself down into the gloom, where he could see a crumbling flight of steps.

Tony stepped down into an underground room with only the tiniest of windows. But the light blazed with the same orangey warmth that he'd seen and felt from below him. Cold stone lined the walls, floor and ceiling of the underground cell. In the middle was a stone table with an empty plate and a carved stone goblet. A heavy, oak chair had been pulled back as if someone had recently finished a meal.

From the gloom in the furthest corner, a thin sparrow-stalk of a boy crouched and peered out at him.

The golden light was coming from the sad creature

himself. He was radiating it. The sound of singing had lessened, as had the tumbling voices in Tony's head. At last he felt that he could think straight. He half expected to see Merlin, or Eleri. He wasn't sure why. That had been Merlin's voice, hadn't it? Telling him to remember the prophecy. The words he didn't know before he spoke them with such power. 'Guess I'm cleverer than I thought,' Tony grinned.

He met the boy's intense blue gaze, one hand shading his eyes. The blaze of light around the child was so great at times that he could only just pick out his features. 'I can see you,' he said, wondering what to say.

'Rescue,' the thin boy replied. And there was that eagerness in the voice again. What if Tony couldn't help? What if he just ended up letting him down?

'You broke open my prison.' The little boy rose as he spoke, and to his horror Tony saw a chain joined to an iron band on his left wrist. It stretched its cold blue-black links as far back as the eye could see.

'Er, yeah, I suppose I did.'

'I called out to you and you came.'

'But I don't know what to do next,' Tony said, frustrated. 'Am I supposed to get you out of here on my own? I thought Merlin and Eleri were going to help me but I've lost them. No. Stop that. Please.' To his embarrassment the thin little figure had thrown himself at his feet. 'You don't have to do that.'

'But you knew them,' the boy beamed up at him. 'You knew the words of power. And you heard my father's lament.'

I'm not sure I did, thought Tony. But maybe that was

what all the wailing had been. Tony had never been good with praise or other people's feelings and now both were being thrown at him at once. He felt like hiding his head in a bucket. 'Look, I don't understand any of this. I'm just . . .'

'But you must,' said the boy with passion. 'You are little Gwern. You're here to set me free.'

CHAPTER SIX

GOLDEN BOY

'Whoa, just wait a minute there. You've got this all wrong. You must have got me mixed up with someone else. I can see that now. I'm not Gwern. My name's Tony. I don't know anything about this. Or,' and he felt bad saying it, 'you. And please get up. It creeps me out when you do that.'

A look of uncertainty came over the boy's face and, for a few brief seconds, he looked disappointed. As he struggled to his feet and backed into the corner, Tony could see how wasted his limbs were. Then his thin features lit up with sudden delight. 'No, it's true. You have come to rescue me. You are Gwern, the Alder boy. You are the one who will give me my real name.'

'No. You've got it wrong. I'm just . . .' The sounds were filling Tony's head again. But there was something else. Something about the paintings his mum had left for him. *Come away from the fire, little Gwern.*

Tony paused. 'Can you see me?'

'I can . . . see . . . you.' The words were squeezed out with some difficulty.

'So you can see in the dark?'

'Some things.' Again the boy's mouth struggled, as if he was chewing on a stuck toffee.

161

'So how long have you been here? And who put you here?'

'I do not know . . . the answer to any of it. I have only been told that I am here and may not go anywhere. And that I must learn my lessons and eat and drink what I am given. Then maybe one day . . .'

The stream fizzled out. It must have been a long speech for him.

'Mother,' the boy said almost in a whisper.

'She isn't here.' Tony didn't know why he said it. He knew it was cruel.

Something unexpected then. A fierce look came into the wasted face and a blush to the cheeks. A knotting of fists like a playground victim who'd been pushed once too often.

Then it was as if the boy remembered, and his whole mood changed like a light going on inside him. A light to match the furry glow that framed his head and shoulders like a lion's mane. Tony was getting used to the way this odd light worked, how it changed with his moods – warm one minute, blazing the next. It was blazing now and he was forced to step back.

'I'm sorry,' Tony tried to say.

'No, I'm the one who's sorry.' The little boy came out of his corner, waving his hand about in an agitated manner, his mane of light glowing warmly. Tony couldn't help noticing the coils of blue-black chain that came with him. The whole thing made him shudder.

'I am sorry your fine clothes are spoilt, sir.'

Tony just looked at him puzzled. 'These aren't fine. They're just some tatty old jeans and T-shirt and you can stop calling me sir.'

'But this is not the way I have been taught to greet guests.' Now the boy had a dirty cloth in his hands and was actually trying to dust Tony down like he was his footman or something.

'No. Stop it.'

'But I must. I forgot myself before. You must forgive me.'

'Stop it!' Tony screamed in his face, yanking the cloth out of his hands and stamping on it.

The boy stopped in shock and then turned away as if from a blow. Then the light blazed around him even fiercer and the heat of it spun Tony to the floor.

'It is usually easier to allow him to do as he wants.'

And there they were: Merlin and Eleri, one tall and frowning, the other pale and smiling.

'You got here then?' the old man grinned, eyeing the sick down Tony's shirt.

'Are you all right?' asked Eleri, more sympathetic.

Strangest of all was the renewed glow on the boy's face. 'Master,' he said, looking at Merlin with grateful wonder. 'I knew you would come for me.'

And instead of shaking his head or arguing as Tony thought he would, Merlin merely smiled at the golden boy. 'Yes,' he answered. 'I said I would, didn't I?'

'Did you?' Tony asked, wondering how he was supposed to keep up.

'But, Merlin, can this really be the time?' The look in Eleri's eyes was anxious. 'He has been promised so many times before. Aren't you just being cruel?'

'I think if recent events teach us anything, it's that moments do not simply come.' Merlin gave a grim smile. 'Sometimes you have to just grab them.'

'So who is he anyway?' Tony said rudely. 'Why does he have to go everywhere with that chain? And why has he got that orange halo thing all round him? How did he get here?'

'Maybe it's time for that as well,' Merlin said. 'This is a very special lad. He is the greatest of us all. The child of light. The Mabon.'

'Mabon,' the boy said and beamed his golden smile.

Maybe he wasn't as unhealthy as all that, Tony thought. Now his eyes had adjusted, and he could see the underground room and some of the things in it. There were books, and a mattress on the floor which did not look too uncomfortable.

'He has been happy in his own way,' Merlin said quietly, answering Tony's unspoken thought.

'But why the chain?' Tony protested. 'That's just well over the top.'

'For his own safety as much as anything.' Merlin smiled and ruffled the little boy's hair, which stood up like a stiff brush. Mabon rubbed his head against Merlin's hand like a pet dog. The whole thing made Tony feel even more uneasy.

'Isn't that right, my boy?'

It felt unreal, as if they'd stepped into some Victorian drawing room where the children were being presented to Papa before bedtime.

'You could always just have trusted him,' Eleri hissed, rather to Tony's surprise. 'There must have been a better way than this.'

'Ah, how naïve, how innocent you sound.'

Now Merlin was showing off, thought Tony.

'Sometimes children need special protection. Don't forget that.'

The words dried in Merlin's throat as he caught sight of Eleri's face, which was white and furious. 'Do forgive me, my dear.' The old man tried to stumble his way out of the crisis. 'I should never have said that to you of all people. Please forgive me.'

He was like a landed fish trying to wriggle off the hook, thought Tony.

'Wonderful. I do so love reunions.' The sound of that familiar smooth-as-silk voice made all of them swing round.

But this was a new Lord Arran, dressed in a black cloak edged in rich sable against which his long silver hair appeared all the more impressive. He carried the staff in his hand as if by right, and the sword at his waist as if he intended to draw it.

Arran's eyes were a blazing, intelligent green and his expression in contrast to Merlin's set face was warm and smiling. 'How are you doing, my fine fellow?' he asked the boy.

He sounds like a character in a book, thought Tony.

'I am fine, thank you, sir,' the child replied, all politeness.

But Merlin wasn't playing the same game. 'What are you doing here?' he said in a voice like trapped ice.

'I? Why, I have come to check on my charge, old man. You are not the only one to imagine you have his welfare at heart.'

Tony cast a glance at Merlin to see whether he believed him.

'You imagine I have not been aware of all the plots

you've been hatching? You, and those old fleabags you serve?'

Merlin stiffened in fury.

But Tony was bothered about something else. 'How did you get out of that fire thing? Edwin?'

Lord Arran smirked in reply and gave a slow handclap. 'I really should have searched you, shouldn't I? I only have myself to blame. But to answer your question: the fire was just a minor inconvenience. And now that you've found your way here, I can deal with your annoying persistence once and for all. You're becoming almost as tiresome as your mother.'

Which was when Tony went for him. Forgetting everything in the white heat of the moment. Swearing in fury as he drew back a hand and smacked the smirking face. Feeling the bruising of his knuckles, but registering the other's discomfort, and that was enough.

'Boy!' Lord Arran snapped.

Mabon came forward, blazing with light, and at last Tony got it. For the first time he could see the real Mabon, the pure light and dangerous power that lay at his heart, and the true reason why he had been kept prisoner all these years. What a deadly weapon he would be if unleashed!

But what was this? The boy had stopped. He was smiling. Lord Arran was smiling and the blaze of light was dazzling. The little Mabon held out a hand to Tony. Uncertain, Tony used his left hand to shield himself, holding out his right.

'Don't touch him,' Merlin screamed.

But it was too late.

CHAPTER SEVEN

TRICKS

Tony didn't have time to worry because the power, the light, whatever it was, was jolting through him. The full power of a little being so dangerous that for his own safety, and everyone else's, he had to be shut away from the world.

The sheer force of the blast threw everyone but the boy and Lord Arran to the stone floor. As Tony scrambled to his feet, he could see Merlin struggling with something. Batting it away as if he was under attack.

It was Eleri that concerned him more. She lay still and cold on the floor and he hadn't even seen her fall.

'Oops,' Lord Arran laughed. 'No one to come to your rescue now, I fear. Time to end this little charade once and for all.'

Tony fought back the angry tears. There was no way he was going to let this man see how upset he was. This man who had bullied and hounded his mother and poor Margaret. This man who had pretended to be Edwin.

But why had he wanted to bring him here?

'You see, Tony,' Lord Arran explained, 'I am actually very impressed with you. For, in my long life, I have faced many foes and hardly any of them have shown such spirit, tenacity and courage as you have. But now it is over. I have you all where I want you.'

'You killed my mother.'

'Indeed I did not.'

That shut him up a bit. 'So why did she have to die then?'

For the first time Tony thought he saw something like kindness in the green eyes, and the voice had softened. 'It was her time, Tony. Sometimes we are at the mercy of greater forces.'

Lord Arran waved his hand and Tony was standing by a hospital bed whose sheets were unnaturally white. The usually bright eyes of the woman lying there were dull and darkened with pain.

One thin hand was doing its best to hold his while he fought back nausea and guilt. He tried to ignore the smell of sickness that seeped under her perfume. There seemed to be tubes everywhere.

It was the only time Tony had been on his own with his dying mother, and he fought the urge to pull away from her. His father and his granddad had just left for the cafeteria, saying they'd be no more than ten minutes. So how was he supposed to tell them he didn't want to be left on his own with her . . . his mum? She was mumbling something that didn't make sense, jabbering on about trees and pictures. She kept repeating the word 'seven'.

Only this time he knew he had to concentrate because she was trying to tell him something. Trying to save him. This time he listened.

'Ask after the Seven.'

Despite the weakness of the whisper he could hear it now.

'Go to the grove, Tony. Call for the princess.'

It was all coming back to him now. How could he not have remembered?

'She will tell you what to do and how to find the rest but you must not let him know.'

'Who?' he remembered asking.

'The silky man. Don't tell him about the Alder boy.'

'Mum. I don't get what you're saying. You're on all kinds of drugs, the doctor says.'

'Tony, you must listen to me.' The grip on his hand was unexpectedly strong.

'Mum, you're scaring me. I don't know about any Alder boy.'

'I have left you the seven but there is an eighth he must not have. The Alder boy is the key.'

'But, Mum, I don't . . .' Tony said, trying to pull both his head and hand away from the painful memory.

'An eighth picture. I knew it,' he heard the triumphant voice of Lord Arran say in the present.

The figure, which had seemed so kind a moment ago, had been replaced by a monster with a mocking smirk whose cold eyes flashed triumph. Arran had tricked him. He had taken him back into his own memories to find out what he wanted to know. Tony didn't believe it was possible to hate anyone so much. How could he have been taken in like that?

Lord Arran had given up all pretence that he was human, looming tall and menacing, his cloak open like the wings of a great black bird, against which the silver-white hair stood out in shocking contrast. The staff cracked down harsh and ringing on the stone floor, and Merlin shrieked, a horrible sound. As Tony looked at him and the still figure of Eleri crouched like a discarded rag doll in the corner, Lord Arran shoved the little boy out of his way, aiming a vicious kick after him.

'Go and serve your true masters,' he snapped and backhanded him across the head. The boy stumbled away while Tony's eyes filled with hot tears at how he had been fooled yet again.

'No more tricks.' Lord Arran was clearly enjoying the power as he looked around him.

'You didn't make much of a show of it in the end,' he smirked. 'I daresay your clod friend and his demented mother could have done better.'

Tony clenched his fists and wished he had half Chris Lord's strength because he'd use it to batter this monster to a pulp.

'The old man was half gone anyway. Living on past glories for far too long. Madness will be nothing new. And, as for the sad princess here, perhaps I should have allowed our friend the butcher the chance to batter a bit more sense into her.'

Any control Tony had snapped at that, and he rushed at him for the second time, fists flailing, legs high-kicking like some crazed martial artist.

Arran laughed and, besides, he didn't look like Arran any more. Who was he, this thing? He was alien, brooding and terrifying. Like a great, dark, winged predator, he scooped up Tony and dangled him with his feet kicking off the floor. Little Mabon stayed mute in his corner.

'You tricked me.' Tony kicked furiously.

'Oh, I tricked you all right, but not just you. All of you. All the way from your precious grove. Would you like me to tell you how? Before I leave you with your new friend? He's been in need of a companion.

'I knew that old fool Merlin and his bird-brained friends would be so tied up with their precious prophecy that they'd find someone to come and rescue our pathetic little prince here. Looks like you drew the short straw. Convenient for me. I can thank that mother of yours for getting you tangled up in it all. Serves her right for not doing the job she was paid for.'

'You planned everything?' Tony swung in the grip of his adversary and did his best to connect with a foot somewhere, but he knew it was futile.

'I planned everything, spitfire, because all you see is mine. Every rock – every tower. I am master of my own realm. It was a simple matter to let a kindle light blow out for you to lose your footing. And to have you call to mind a prophecy. Clever that, don't you think?

'So, having conveniently separated all of you it was then far too easy to arrange this happy reunion of ours. One dead, one mad and the third a prisoner. Not bad?

'You did everything I wanted, with the added bonus that you believed you were doing good. Whatever good is. The brat here made you use your special powers to awaken the grove to draw in the others. Like obedient little soldiers in a row. And that tiresome farm girl had already conveniently opened the gateway between the worlds. Which I always thought would be the hardest bit.'

Lord Arran laughed at that. A hard laugh with no humour in it.

As Tony stood there, helpless, two things happened. First the familiar sensation of dark wings brushing just behind him. There for no more than a second. Then a half-familiar voice came into his head. 'Play the fool,' it said.

Voices

He looked in the direction of the only source the voice could have come from, trying not to signal any change or interest.

Merlin still struggled with wide mad eyes against the pain of his invisible bonds. The golden boy crouched on his sacking and stared at his master. Did he hate him? Or did he love him? And as for poor Eleri?

Tony waited for the voice to come again but there was nothing. Meanwhile Arran was staring at him.

'So what are you going to do with me?' he finally asked.

'Play the fool I tell you,' the voice crackled in his head again, and he nearly told it to shut up. But there was another brief flutter of wings and with that came a strange excitement. He remembered that he wasn't entirely without help here.

'Well,' he began carefully, 'if you're going to keep me here you could at least tell me why. I'm just a kid whose mum left him some crazy paintings, who can do some kind of weird singing that opens doors. I mean you're treating me like I'm some sort of enemy. You only have to look at me to know I'm not.'

Lord Arran let him drop to the ground at last, his legs tangled underneath. He would have a whacking bruise on his knee but what did he care? Arran was giving him a different kind of look. Appraising him.

'Good. Good.' The voice in his head was almost admiring. 'Get him to take you outside. It is your only hope. And ours to help you.'

Tony was torn between laughing at this mad suggestion and relief at realising who was trying to help him. But they could fly, couldn't they? If they wanted to help him, or Merlin and Eleri for that matter. Why weren't they here?

'He has power over this realm, Tony. But the sea is a different matter.'

But why would I want to get near the sea? He almost said it out loud. *What good would that do?*

'The little boy will show you the way,' said the kindest of the voices.

'If you are hoping this stupidity will help you, then you're more of a fool than I took you for,' snapped Lord Arran.

Tony's voice was more careless than he felt. 'If I've got to stay here, then I'd like to see the castle properly. I mean, I'm not seeing much of it underground. Couldn't you show me what it's like up top? If I'm going to be stuck here it's the least you can do.'

Tony almost heard the applause, as if all the heroes who'd ever used some clever delaying tactics had inspired him. But would it work?

Then he became aware of a groaning coming from the corner and could see that little Mabon was doubled over with pain and was clutching hold of the scarred old table for support. He was trying to get to his feet but sank back

174

down almost immediately, his face clouded and creased with effort.

Arran drew back his hand to strike but Tony pulled the boy out of the way. The child fell to the stone floor and half took Tony with him.

'Please,' he still seemed to say, his teeth set against the pain.

'What's up with him?' Tony hissed at Arran, his fear disappearing by the minute.

'Please.' Suddenly the boy pulled away from him and struggled back towards his corner. But was it possible, that before he did so, he looked at Tony with a clear-eyed stare . . . and winked?

'Perhaps he needs some air,' Tony suggested. 'I could come with you. After all I'm not likely to get away, am I . . . in the middle of nowhere?'

'Ask him to do it now.' The voice was almost deafening.

'Why don't you show me now?' he said, suddenly bold. 'He could get some fresh air and you can tell me a bit about the towers and other stuff.'

'Please,' the Mabon said quietly and, without caring what Arran thought, Tony helped him up and supported him under his left arm.

Lord Arran gave no reply but instead looked from one to the other. Then he nodded and unhooked a great rusty key from the iron ring on the wall. It was the first time Tony had noticed it. There were many other keys on the ring and he wondered what they could all be for.

He saw that part of the floor sloped upwards into a series of protuberances which were not quite steps.

Climbing these, Lord Arran stretched up into the hard stone with his right arm and located the spot he was looking for, and then . . . the whole of the roof opened above them, and the cold roar of the sea flooded their senses.

Tony had never felt anything so cold. Even the freezing tombs had been warm in comparison, and he was quickly conscious of how little he was wearing.

'Before you think about trying any tricks,' Arran said, 'be aware that there is only the sea around and beneath us. It has a killing cold which would finish you within seconds. You might be glad to stay inside after all. He is used to it, as am I. You with your loose modern clothes are not.'

Tony nearly lost his chance. He nearly turned and said, 'No, you take him.'

Then the kindest of the voices came into his head. 'Do not fear the cold. I will keep you warm enough but you must appear weak . . . you understand?'

'Tell him about the other thing,' snapped the first voice. Tony was finding it easier to tell them apart. Again he had to fight the urge to answer the questions out loud.

'He needs only to leave the way open,' the second voice tried to butt in.

'Come on then,' snapped Lord Arran. 'Or have you lost all that confidence now?' He had used the same key to loosen the chain and Tony shivered at its weight as the boy shook himself free.

'Oh, shut up,' said Tony out loud and as much to the voices as Lord Arran. 'I'm coming. And I'm bringing him with me.'

'Well done,' said the second voice admiringly. Tony followed Lord Arran's lead by pulling himself up on his hands and wriggling out onto the roof of the world. Squatting up there, he reached down a hand to help the eager little boy to do the same, while Arran stood high and arrogant, surveying his kingdom.

They were on a raised wall which jutted far out to sea. The Mabon's lonely prison of cold stone lay at the beginning, and once they were beyond it there was hardly room for two to walk side by side. The stone was lashed and beaten by the waves and Tony could not imagine walking far without being washed off by their fury. So this, he thought in horror, was the one place the little boy was allowed to walk.

He was so cold and awed that he almost forgot why they had come. That was until he heard the splash.

He turned back and saw the boy struggling in the water. 'He's fallen in,' he shouted to Lord Arran, expecting panic at the escape of his charge.

'Why, naturally,' came the smooth reply. 'How else would you expect him to get his exercise?'

The golden child wasn't struggling in the icy waves at all. He was swimming like a fish.

CHAPTER NINE

DYLAN OF THE WAVES

Tony gaped at him. He had never been a strong swimmer, and could just about keep himself afloat with breast stroke. The little boy was having the time of his life and Tony could see that he was in his element. It was his equivalent of a walk in the exercise yard.

'It's hard to get him out more often than not.' For a few moments it felt almost matey as they stood and watched the boy dive and play.

'Decided not to risk it?' asked Lord Arran with heavy sarcasm.

'How can he swim when I can hardly speak?' In the cold, Tony struggled to form the words, remembering the act he was supposed to be playing. At the same time he was waiting for the voices to return, no matter how irritating or squabbling they might be.

'You – you were g-g-going to tell me about the t-towers,' he stumbled.

'Was I? I think not. Knowledge is power, and I have given you too much of that already.'

'That one will tell you nothing,' the voice came back suddenly in his head and Tony thought it was the second, argumentative voice.

'You must get him out of his element,' said the third.

'Run and take him by surprise,' snapped the impatient first, the one that sounded like a head teacher.

Tony hesitated then, staring out across the churning grey waters and imagining what it would be like to make the one slip that would send a useless swimmer like him down into the depths. He was still finding it far too cold, despite the protective magic.

'Now, Tony. We are with you.'

He nearly answered out loud and gave the game away. Instead, something, maybe it was the gentle tone of the third voice, made him turn round.

Three huge ravens perched on top of the stone roof of the underground prison where Merlin was still held in Lord Arran's enchantment and Eleri might be lying dead. They were the same three battered old birds with their raggedy wings that had squawked at him in the sea cave of Uffern.

Tony looked at the ravens, and then at little Mabon laughing and splashing in the water, and finally at the smirk on his enemy's face.

Then he ran. Skidding and hurtling. Not knowing where he was going and terrified with every step. The ravens watched him and gronked their approval.

Arran roared his rage and, as they had intended he would, came flying after him, his speed breathtakingly quick, almost enough to catch him before he'd even begun.

As he turned to see the fury in the face of his silver-haired pursuer, and hear the hollow ring of his staff on the stones, Tony slipped and more or less cartwheeled head first into the sea.

As long as he lived he would never forget that killing cold. Gasping, he sank like a stone, before kicking instinctively upwards through the bone-numbing water to briefly break the surface, crying and gasping for breath. But the pull of the waves was so hard he knew he could never keep it up.

As he went down for the second time and tried hard to hold his breath against the fierce rush of icy cold, Tony remembered something. He pushed himself upwards, knowing he wouldn't get that strength a third time, and a name came to him from nowhere, like the prophecy had done.

As the ravens watched and waited, and Arran's thunderous face spat fury, Tony screamed it out into the water. 'Dylan,' he cried. 'Dylan of the Waves.'

And the little boy turned in the middle of his water play, and swam joyfully towards him.

At the same time, the three ravens flew wheeling and dipping towards the tall figure glowering on the end of the stone quay. They dived, screaming for his eyes, as a gigantic figure rose from the turbulent waves. Seaweed formed his green crown and streamed off him like a ragged emerald robe. Green fire was in his eyes, and he carried in his mighty gnarled left hand a weapon that was more like a spear than a trident.

The little swimmer reached Tony and pulled him from the water with one hand, and then drew him onto his back while Tony shivered, struggling to stay conscious.

Screams split the air above them as the three ravens attacked. The tall figure in their midst tumbled down into the waters, protecting his eyes with his hands.

The ravens let him go. Screaming with rage and pain, he plummeted into the water. That was when the great sea god reached down his right hand with rough coral bracelets clashing together on his wrist.

Tony tried not to look, certain of the other's horrible end. But something unexpected passed between the two figures. One minute the sea god was grasping Lord Arran in his mighty fist. Next there was a flash of red and silver like a brilliant firework, and Lord Arran was . . . gone.

CHAPTER TEN

Return to the Sea

Merlin stood on the edge of the stone quay. He and the shimmering little boy, who now seemed as much fish as human, helped Tony up to safety.

Merlin looked remarkably unscathed as, with blue eyes sparkling, he cracked his staff down on the stones. A great roaring fire sprang up between him and Tony.

'It will dry you out and restore your senses,' he said gravely. 'Such foolhardy bravery can have a price.'

'Wh— how did you get out?' stammered Tony. If he hadn't been shivering quite so much he might almost have been annoyed. 'I thought he had you in some spell.'

'Oh, he might have thought so, but you have to get up early to get the better of me. Mind you, it did help, you distracting him like that. You're more use than you look, aren't you?'

Tony grinned at that. The old cheeky Merlin was back. 'Yeah, it's good to see you too,' he said, looking at the clotted dark red of the water.

The great seaweed-clad figure, silent until now, to Tony's surprise, spoke to him directly. 'Thank you. Thank you,' he said in a voice raw with emotion. 'For rescuing him at last.'

Tony gasped as he looked from one to the other, and then as the little one they had called Mabon shyly took his hand, he struggled to explain. 'I thought he rescued me. It's me who should be saying "thank you". What did I do?'

'You gave him his name back,' Merlin said solemnly. 'And that freed him. He can return home now; his father has waited a long time for him.'

'Dylan of the Waves,' Tony repeated the name. He half stumbled when he tried to get up, and it was then that he saw the three women standing behind Merlin.

'But then there's so much I don't understand. Why was he a prisoner? Why was I the one to rescue him? What's it got to do with the Seven? Or the Guardians? And why did he call me Gwern?'

He looked across at the little boy as if expecting him to answer. Then he looked back at the women.

Women. They looked more like queens with not even a hint of the tatty raven about them, and, outside the gloom of the cave of Uffern, he saw them clearly for the first time. They were all tall, beautiful, otherworldly.

The dark one seemed the eldest; she had the hardest, thinnest face and black hair. She wore silver and black, and her eyes were coals blazing.

The second had fierce green eyes and hair like a helmet of fire; she wore a red-and-silver gown. The third one, the one with the gentle voice, had deep blue eyes, soft golden curls and a dress of emerald.

Tony gaped at them as the third queen spoke. 'It is not over, Tony. You must now return to your own world and make yourself ready. You must go back. The Seven must

183

gather so that the Guardians may awaken and the prophecy be fulfilled.'

Not much, then, thought Tony.

They were all speaking now and Tony wanted to smile because the warmth of their voices made him feel safe and happy. But their words were hard and confusing and he found himself getting angry again. As usual nothing made sense. No one was telling him anything. It didn't help that he was shivering with the cold.

'And I'm supposed to understand it just like that, am I? I don't even know what the prophecy is. Or how to find the rest of the Seven. You all expect me to know stuff, and I don't. You're just like teachers who don't like my homework answers.'

Tony saw two of the queens smile at that.

'The gods forbid that anyone should ever think me a teacher, Tony.' Merlin gave him a wolfish grin.

But Tony ignored him. 'So what is this prophecy?' He addressed his question to the three queens. 'And what does it have to do with me?'

The answer came from none of them. Instead Merlin raised his staff again and cracked it down hard onto the stone of the causeway. Blue fire spat and sparked from the end. With a mighty roar, a great rock powered its way to the surface of the sea, displacing the grey water all around it. The rock looked older than old, pitted and scarred with seaweed and algae.

On the stone was ancient writing. Tony read aloud:

> 'Who will take the Seven home
> And bring the Dark Lord from his throne?

Who will show the Mage the skies
And bring the Bard an end to lies?
Who will raise the Ship again
And free the Princess from her pain?
Who will teach the Lost to fight
And bring the Child into the light?'

Tony looked at the green-black lettering, which somehow still seemed to be part of the rock. 'But those are the words I spoke, aren't they?' he muttered.

'You used them to rescue me, Tony.' Dylan had put his hand shyly in his, but Tony could see that he was looking wistfully out into the still-churning sea. Towards the rock and the great seaweed-draped figure who stood beside it.

'That's the prophecy, Tony.' It was the gentle voice of the golden queen.

'So how am I supposed to fulfil it? Me and the rest of the Seven?'

'The last part of it, the most important part, you have completed with the rescue of Dylan,' the queen continued. 'And other parts are coming together. Your friendship, for example, is doing a great deal to help the healing of a princess.'

'Eleri, is she . . . ?'

'With rest, she will be fine, Tony.' It was Merlin who reassured him this time.

'But what about the ship and the bard and the rest of it?'

'They are not tasks for you alone,' said the red-haired queen, 'although the finding of the lost ship will one day be part of your destiny.'

'And Lord Arran, he's trying to stop this prophecy? That's what he's up to. Why did you let him go?'

Tony saw the queens exchange glances with Merlin. They seemed uncertain.

'He has been allowed to go his own way for now, Tony,' the dark one said at last. 'But he will come back. He will regain his strength.'

'But it was dead cool what you did. Looked like you almost blinded him.'

'Hush, Tony,' scolded the blonde queen. 'A friend wants to say farewell.'

The little boy, Dylan, was looking up at Tony with wonder and love, before squeezing his hand for a final time. 'When you are ready you must send for me,' he said. Then as Tony looked after him in bafflement he ran still dripping to the edge of the rock, before diving into the welcoming sea and towards the joyful arms of a father who had waited so long for his return.

'What did he mean by that?' he muttered.

Then Tony watched as the sea king gathered the thin little boy in his arms and gently cradled him. He looked first to Merlin, and then back to the three queens. The sight of the little boy and his father had brought back memories of his own family and he was suddenly homesick. Tony stood there for a while, feeling small and lost and a little out of place. He shivered as the cold bit through his thin shirt and trousers.

'So what am I expected to do now?' he said at last.

'You will know, Tony,' the dark one spoke, her voice unexpectedly kind. Then she looked at her sisters. Their hands flashed silver fire and streams of red and gold till they met in a single stream of white fire crackling all around him.

As Tony looked for a last time at the joyful sight of father and son romping in the fresh waves of their reunion, Merlin crashed down his staff again. 'Farewell, Tony,' he called.

Just before the spell began to take effect, Tony saw a familiar figure at Merlin's shoulder. She looked thin and shaky but he recognised her all right.

'Eleri!' he shouted joyfully.

'Farewell, Tony,' called both Merlin and Eleri, and as he saw her smile he felt an emptiness in his stomach. It felt as if he was losing more than he knew.

'You will find your way sooner than you think,' the third queen called after him.

'I was just going to come out to look for you. When did you sneak back in?'

'Dad!'

Tony was sitting in his mum's half of the studio with the paintings spread out in front of him. He tried not to look startled.

'I might have guessed. We're waiting on supper for you so you might as well come down and have it. Sophie and I are ravenous.'

'Er, yeah. Sure, Dad.'

'Talk to your friend, did you? That Edwin bloke?'

How was he supposed to answer that one?

'Well, maybe it's time you fixed your eyes on something

else. You've had enough of all that stuff for now. Which reminds me, that big lad phoned. He called a couple of times when you were ill too.'

'Chris? You never said, Dad. What about him?'

'Well, you'll be making more sense of it than me, I'm sure. The boy sounded out of breath.'

'What did he say, Dad?'

'He said "Tell Clogger I'm fine and so's Mam".'

'That's great then,' Tony smiled. 'That's good news.'

'Makes sense to you, does it?'

'Yeah, it does, Dad.'

'Good. Now come on. Sophie's starving.'

Thanks to:
John and Caitlin; Jennifer Hutchinson;
my patient parents, Pat and Wray Gladwin;
Kevin Crossley-Holland; the ladies of Bereaved Friends;
Rosie; and my dear Aunt Lucy for sharing her precious
marmalade recipes